D0977413

MINERVA CLARK

gives up the ghost

Also by Karen Karbo

Minerva Clark Gets a Clue

Minerva Clark Goes to the Dogs

MINERVA CLARK

gives up *the* ghost

by KAREN KARBO

Published by Bloomsbury U.S.A. Children's Books
175 Fifth Avenue, New York, NY 10010
Distributed to the trade by Holtzbrinck Publishers

Library of Congress Cataloging-in-Publication Data
Karbo, Karen.
Minerva Clark gives up the ghost : a Minerva Clark mystery / by Karen Karbo.—1st U.S. ed.
p. cm.
Summary: Thirteen-year-old amateur sleuth Minerva Clark is contacted by a boy whose parents' Portland, Oregon, grocery store burned down, but when she agrees to investigate the fire, she does not expect to become an arson suspect herself.
ISBN-13: 978-1-58234-679-3 • ISBN-10: 1-58234-679-8
[1. Arson—Fiction. 2. Family life—Portland (Or.)—Fiction. 3. Portland (Or.)—Fiction. 4. Mystery and detective stories.] I. Title.
PZ7.K132Mj 2007 [Fic]—dc22 2007015091

First U.S. Edition 2007
Typeset by Westchester Book Composition
Printed in the U.S.A. by Quebecor World Fairfield
2 4 6 8 10 9 7 5 3 1

For Fiona

– 1 –

The day Angus Paine called, I was at the mall with my mother—known to the rest of the world as Mrs. Dagnitz—shopping for something to wear to her wedding reception. We were in Claire's, searching for the perfect necklace to go with my perfect new halter dress. My mom's favorite word is "perfect." My new halter dress was a dark chocolate brown with big, pale pink polka dots. My oldest older brother, Mark Clark, who was normally in charge of me, would never have bought me this dress. He would have thought it was too grown-up and expensive. But Mrs. Dagnitz was trying to suck up to me because she left our family and moved to Santa Fe. Of course, I let her. What else was I supposed to do?

I wandered around Claire's. The place was crowded with pairs of chirpy girlfriends, girls and their bored boyfriends, and a little girl sitting in a high white-leather chair, kicking her legs, too young to be afraid of the ear-piercing coming her way.

I refused to look at the necklaces. I was in a moody freak mood. Mrs. Dagnitz and Mr. Dagnitz had already had one wedding reception for their yoga vegetarian friends in Santa Fe, but they could not just leave it at that. She needed to drag Mr. Dagnitz all the way to where we lived in Portland, Oregon, for a second wedding reception. She had told Mark Clark that she thought it was time we all began bonding. When Mr. Dagnitz was just plain old Weird Rolando, with his man braid and yoga pants, my brothers and I weren't required to bond. Now it was a whole new deal. Now, on her side of the family, we were blended, and she needed to organize an extra wedding reception to rub it in.

I looked at the rubber glow-in-the-dark MP3 cases. They felt strange, like what I imagine a corpse would feel like. I've never touched a corpse and I don't have an MP3 player. I used to like that I didn't have one, thought it made me deep. Now I wanted one. I wanted to *have* one, right that minute. I didn't want to wait for my birthday, which was coming up in exactly twenty-three days.

"How about this?" said Mrs. Dagnitz. She stood in front of the necklace wall at the back of the store, fingering a gold chain. "Now that's cute—it's a guitar pick. On a chain. It's fourteen-karat gold . . . isn't that sweet?

Isn't that sort of perfect? A guitar-pick necklace. They have them in tortoiseshell and black. Should we get one of each?"

Mrs. Dagnitz's other hand rested on her skinny waist. I used to love that she was a trim, athletic mom. Now I think it wouldn't kill her to act her age, which is old. There should be a rule that when a girl becomes a teen, her mom has to stop shopping in the Junior section. Mrs. Dagnitz was wearing a pair of white shorts, a tank top, and some ancient blue leather Birkenstocks she used to garden in, back when she was still married to my dad and had the last name of Clark, like the rest of us. Her toenails were painted mint green.

"Minnow?" she called out as she looked around for me.

I hated it when my mother called me Minnow. I am three inches taller than her with about ten times as much hair. She was the minnow.

"These necklaces—aren't they just adorable?" she called out in a louder voice. Like I hadn't heard her the first time.

"I don't play the guitar," I said.

"I don't think that really matters. It's sassy, don't you think?"

Sassy? Was Mrs. Dagnitz *trying* to make my head explode from pure irritation?

Mrs. Dagnitz fished the necklace off the hook where it was hanging and checked the price. "It'd look cute with your little halter dress. I love what that dress does for your hair. It really brings the red out. You should always consider dark brown to be your black. The way other girls have little black dresses? You should have little dark brown dresses."

I thought, *Yeah, I'll get right on that.*

To be fair, Mrs. Dagnitz was doing her best to be nice.

I shuffled toward the necklace wall, stopping to gaze with fake interest at a twirling rack that displayed nothing but headbands. Then at some bracelets made of plastic beads that looked like green grapes. Then a rhinestone tiara.

Mrs. Dagnitz stood in front of the necklace wall and waited. She didn't even tap her foot. She was really trying. I gave it another twelve hours, and that was if the heat wave broke. By ten A.M., according to the radio, it was already a hundred out. I stuck the tiara on my head.

"Look, I'm a princess," I said.

Mrs. Dagnitz threw her head back and laughed. I sighed. It wasn't that funny. It wasn't funny at all, in fact. I was hoping to lure her into saying something so lame I could get away with rolling my eyes. But no. What was going on? Why was she being so patient and weird? Maybe it was because she was in love (with Mr. Dagnitz). I was also in love (with Kevin), but I wasn't in such a bombdiggity great mood.

Suddenly, from behind the cash register the counter

girl called out, "I gotta ask—aren't you Minerva Clark?"

"Uh . . . I am. How did you know?" I snatched the tiara off my head and slung it back on its hook. I walked over to where she was rearranging some rings inside a plastic case. She kept moving them around long after they looked as if they were in order. I could tell she was nervous.

"You're famous, girlfriend!" she said. The cashier was tall, with short, dyed-orange hair. She had a gold ring dangling from beneath her button nose. Her name tag said "Scarecrow."

"Famous?"

"Well, not like Brad Pitt. But famous around here." Scarecrow giggled. She *was* nervous.

The only thing I could imagine is that she'd read the story about my last mystery in the Sunday newspaper.

"Check it out." She waved me around the counter. Her perfume smelled like lemon pie. Sure enough, taped to the side of the cash register was a copy of the story. The headline said something dorky about Portland's Own Nancy Drew. There was a color picture of me standing in my driveway in front of my bike, attempting to cuddle Jupiter beneath my chin. I tried to tell the photographer that ferrets were many things, but cuddlers they were not. He didn't care. He snapped away as Jupiter snaked around and tried to bite my thumb.

In the story, the reporter called me "a unique 'tween with a flair for solving mysteries," and told how I'd cracked an identity-theft ring, caught a murderer, and then gone on to help esteemed local jeweler Louis de Guzman recover a rare red diamond, stolen during his return to Portland from London.

Don't believe everything you read. The reporter got it all wrong. I solved the mystery of who stole the diamond, but the gem was gone for good. Also, I am thirteen, which is not a 'tween but a full-blooded teenager.

The story also talked about the electric shock that nearly killed me. Also not true. An electric shock had not nearly killed me, but it had done some weird things with my mind. Like just about every teenage girl, I used to despise myself. Now, for a reason that no one could explain, I thought I was okay just the way I was. Because I wasn't thinking about how I appeared to people all the time, I was more perceptive than the average kid. I could see what was going on with people. They quoted Dr. Lozano, the children's brain expert who examined me after my accident, about how unusual I was, about how she'd had only one other patient like me, ever.

"We have been totally swamped since this story came out," said Scarecrow.

She pointed to a sentence someone had highlighted with neon-green highlighter. It said how Louis de Guzman had replaced the glass center stone in his daughter's ring with the red diamond, for purposes of transporting it into the country from London, and that the ring had come from Claire's.

"At least once a day I get someone asking if we have that same ring. What's with that?"

"They probably think there might just be a million-dollar diamond accidentally stuck in the middle of it." My other idea was that people were basically crazy.

"What's going on?" said Mrs. Dagnitz, suddenly appearing at my shoulder. She wore the same clean-sheets-smelling perfume she'd worn since I was a little girl. For some reason, I found this annoying.

"Nothing," I said.

Scarecrow opened her mouth, probably to tell Mrs. Dagnitz the same thing she'd just told me, but before she could speak, my cell rang—*Oooo-oooo-oooo-ahhnn!* Thumpa-thumpa-thumpa. *Oooo-oooo-oooo-ahhnn!* Thumpa-thumpa-thumpa.

"Good Lord!" said Mrs. Dagnitz. She was so startled by my new ring tone—a wild gorilla beating her chest—that she hopped back and clean out of one of her Birkenstocks. She fell sideways and grabbed my arm. I rolled my eyes. I got the ring tone from my best friend, Reggie, who got it from a guy he knows who works at some world-famous zoo.

"It's just a gorilla, Mom. Jeez!"

"You about gave me a heart attack," Mrs. Dagnitz said, rolling *her* eyes. "There isn't a nice little tune you could use for a ring tone?"

No, Mommie dearest, there is no nice little tune. I flipped open my phone.

Scarecrow smiled at my mother's total lameness and asked if she could ring up the guitar-pick necklace.

"Is this Minerva Clark?" asked the quiet voice on my phone. It was halting and soft. I couldn't tell if it was a boy or a girl until it flew up and squeaked at the end of the sentence. It was a boy, about my age.

"What?" I asked. "I can't hear you."

The caller cleared his throat. "I'm looking for Minerva Clark."

"This is Minerva. But you're going to have to talk louder."

"I need a mystery solved."

Excitement whirled in my stomach. Could this be the beginning of my real sleuthing career? I had stumbled upon my first mystery by accident, and my second mystery involved helping Louis de Guzman's daughter, Chelsea, who was in my class at school. To be a real sleuth I needed strangers to call me up and seek my help.

"Who is it?" said Mrs. Dagnitz, pawing through her huge purse in search of her wallet. Mrs. Dagnitz carried the biggest purse in the nation. You could lose a ham in that purse. I turned away from the counter and strolled back across the store, stopping in front of a rack of beaded bracelets.

"Do I know you?" I asked the caller. I stood with my back to my mother, my finger pressed to my nonphone ear, just so I could hear. Mark Clark would have nailed me to the floor for being rude.

"I don't think we've ever met," said the voice. "My name is Angus Paine. Have you ever been to Corbett Street Grocery? It's my family's store."

"Sounds familiar," I said.

"We're one of the stops on Cryptkeeper Ron's Tour of Haunted Portland. Have you been on the tour or heard of it?"

"Sure," I said. "My brothers took me on it around Halloween a couple of years ago." I didn't remember any haunted grocery stores. There were about six stops on the tour, but the one that stuck with me most was the haunted elementary school, where the boys' bathroom was haunted by a kid who'd drowned when a group of older boys had stuck his head in the toilet.

"Our ghost lives in the walk-in freezer," said Angus Paine.

"Cool," I said. "Ha ha."

Either Angus Paine didn't get the pun, or else he wasn't in a laughing mood.

"Or she did, anyway," he said. "We're not sure she's even there anymore."

"Oh," I said, thinking, *Please tell me that Angus Paine is not going to ask me to use my Ouija board to find his lost ghost.*

"Someone set the grocery on fire," said Angus Paine. "The only thing left is the back wall."

"And you want me . . ."

". . . to help me find out who did it. This grocery has been in our family for almost a hundred years. If I can trouble you to meet me, I'll show you the damage. If we don't get an insurance settlement for arson, my dad says we won't be able to rebuild it."

"Well . . . ," I said. I cradled the phone on my shoulder. I didn't know one thing about arson, and the whole topic of insurance just shouted Boring Adult Business. I teased an orange plastic bracelet off one of the hooks and slipped it on my wrist. Even though we Clarks are tall and strong, we have dainty wrists.

I glanced around. Mrs. Dagnitz was coming toward me. She paused to fish for her sunglasses in her purse. After we were finished at Claire's we needed to stop at Whole Foods for the organic spinach she needed to make her vegetarian lasagna for Mark Clark's birthday dinner, which was still a few days away, and then at some special store where they sell only fish. We needed to stop somewhere else for something else, too. Something to do with aromatherapy. I closed my eyes. After my mom left my dad and moved to Santa Fe, I spent a year wanting her to come back. Now I wished she would go back to Santa Fe. Having her home was exhausting, and not in a fun way.

"If it's not something you think you can help me with, I understand completely," said Angus Paine. "Arson is difficult to prove. And, you don't know me."

"How *did* you find out about me?" I asked.

"The story in the paper," he said.

"But how did you get my number?"

"Dialed Information, of course. There aren't too many Minerva Clarks in Portland."

"Like, zero," I said.

"Don't be so sure." All of a sudden his soft voice turned sharp and mean, as if he'd handed off the phone to some evil twin. "I know you're a smart one, but you're not as smart as you think. There actually *is* another Minerva Clark. She's about ninety and raises potbellied pigs. I had a nice chat with her."

"O-kaay," I said. What was his problem? So there was another Minerva Clark in town.

"There's one other thing you should know," said Angus. He'd calmed down. His sweet, polite voice returned. "Grams Lucille died in the fire. She lived upstairs, over the store. They found her sitting straight up in her favorite chair, completely burned. Her polyester pants were melted to her chair."

"Oh jeez," I said.

"The store just smelled like burned wood and electrical wires and melted plastic. But in Grams Lucille's apartment it smelled—"

"I get the picture," I said. "That's awful."

"It is," he said. "That's why I hope you can help me. I hope to talk to you again."

Then I heard dead space. A strange boy called with a

strange mystery for me to solve, then hung up on me just like that. Instantly, I wished I'd been friendlier, wished I'd said yes to Angus Paine and his burned-down family grocery store.

I whirled around and Mrs. Dagnitz was standing about two inches away from me, hands on hips, giant purse slung over one shoulder. How much of the conversation she'd heard I hadn't a clue. I don't know why I didn't want Mrs. Dagnitz to hear my conversations. I gave in to the sudden urge to lean over and shake out my hair. The thought of a new mystery—I knew already that I would call Angus Paine back, and soon—made my wild hair stick to my head, even in Claire's über-air-conditioning.

"Was that Kevin on the phone?" Mrs. Dagnitz asked as we left the store.

"No," I said. "Not really."

"Not really?" Mrs. Dagnitz laughed. "What does that mean?"

Claire's is on the third floor of the mall. We approached the first of two down escalators and I wiped my sweaty palms on my thighs. I hate down escalators. They are evil incarnate. The steps look as if they disappear into a parallel world. Maybe they do. Maybe every time you hop on a down escalator, you're being deposited into a world that seems familiar but really contains new freakish realities, like your mother, who doesn't even live with you, who doesn't have any business butting into your private life, grilling you like a police detective about your personal phone calls.

Mrs. Dagnitz and I rode the escalators to the bottom floor, one after the other. I tried not to look down. I held on to the rubber railing until I got a cramp in my hand. I was not about to grab her arm and show what a baby I was.

All the while, Mrs. Dagnitz kept asking how I had met Kevin (at the indoor water park, with my friend Hannah), how old he was (fourteen going on fifteen, one year older than me, almost exactly), where he went to high school (Jesuit), what his father did (how am I supposed to know).

"You don't know what his father does?" she asked as we left the mall and plunged into the parking structure. It was hot and smelled of car exhaust and something sweet and rotten. Mrs. Dagnitz forgot where we had parked. We walked up and down the aisles. She turned her head this way and that, checking out every big white SUV we passed. She mumbled to herself, "I can't believe I forgot where I parked the car. Why do I always do this?"

I was on the verge of moaning that my feet hurt, or complaining about the smell or the heat, but all of a sudden I felt bad for my mom. I could see her blond bangs sticking to her sweaty forehead. She was frantic. By the time I get old, there will be pills to prevent you from losing track of where you parked your enormous white car.

"It wasn't Kevin anyway," I said. "It was some boy named Angus who needs a mystery solved." The instant that leaped out of my mouth, I knew it was a mistake.

At that moment we found the car, parked between two other white SUVs, on the ramp between the first and second floor. Mrs. Dagnitz said nothing. She opened her car door, slid inside, then reached over and unlocked my door. I got in. Mrs. Dagnitz was still dead quiet. She flipped the air-conditioning on high, and we roared off down the ramp. I reached over and turned on the radio. Mrs. Dagnitz reached over and turned it off. Uh-oh. A parent turning off the radio instead of turning it down can mean only one thing.

"I wanted to talk to you about all this nosing around you've been doing," she said.

I rolled my lips inside my mouth and stared out the window at a Goth couple strolling into a 7-Eleven. I was not going to say a word. I turned the air-conditioning vent on my face, closed my eyes, and tried to focus on the dry, cool air blowing on my cheeks. My mom was an expert at saying the same thing over and over until finally you agreed with her just to get her to stop. Trying to tell your side of things only made the whole ordeal twice as long.

"Poking around into other people's business is just

asking for trouble. Not only that, it's dangerous and you could get hurt," she said.

I looked out the window.

"That's what they have police detectives for, Minnow," she said.

More looking out the window.

"That's what they get paid for, solving crimes. You keep this up and one day you'll find yourself in jail or . . . or worse!"

"Does the air inside the car get colder if you drive faster?" I finally asked.

"I'm serious, Minerva! This is not something you want to be doing. Life isn't a movie. What if you discover some drug addict is involved in one of these crimes? Those people don't mess around. They have guns."

"I'm serious, too. Quills told me how air-conditioning worked once, but I forgot."

"Next time please do me a favor and just call the police. Just have that Angus person call the police."

"All right, fine."

"Promise me."

"I said 'fine,' all right?"

The air-conditioning whirred as we tooled along in silence. I dared to imagine the conversation was over, reached over, and turned the radio back on.

"I just think there are other ways you can use your . . . new gifts," she said.

"What new gifts?" I asked, just to be dense. I sank down in my seat and propped my knees against the dashboard. Mrs. Dagnitz and I had never really talked about the way I'd changed since my accident. I looked over at her. I couldn't imagine what she was going to say.

"It's just so nice to see you with all this self-confidence. You should take advantage of it. Have *fun*, enjoy it. I was thinking we could get your hair straightened. And I'd like to buy you some kicky sandals. Those tennis shoes you like are adorable, but you're old enough to learn about the world of shoes."

"The *world* of shoes?" I snorted.

"Maybe you could straighten your hair before school starts. They have that new Japanese method. It'd be fun."

"Fun? How is straightening your hair fun? That's like saying going to the dentist is fun."

"Going to the dentist can be fun . . . having healthy, white, perfect teeth can make you feel good about your smile. And a pretty smile does wonders for your self-esteem."

That word hung in the car like a huge invisible air freshener hanging from the rearview mirror. "I already *have* self-esteem," I said. "Straight Japanese hair wouldn't make me have more of it."

"I said it was a method perfected by the Japanese," said Mrs. Dagnitz, running a yellow light.

"Mark Clark says you can get a ticket for that."

"All I'm trying to say is that you're young, Minnow. You've got your entire life ahead of you, and you just shouldn't be afraid to . . . what's the word you kids use? Work it."

"That would be two words," I said.

"You understand what I'm getting at?"

"Yeah," I said. "Instead of doing something *interesting* I should be obsessed with trying to look like Paris Hilton."

"I am NOT saying that at all," said Mrs. Dagnitz.

She lies.

"Thank you. Drive through, please." I couldn't believe I had said this to my mother. Mark Clark would have grounded me straight into the afterlife if I had said that to him.

"I just want you to be happy!" she cried.

"I am happy," I said. *Until you showed up*, I wanted to say, but even I am not that mean. Luckily, we'd arrived at Whole Foods. Mrs. Dagnitz parked in the space farthest from the door.

"There's a space over there," I said, even though I couldn't have cared less.

"I try to get in as much walking as possible during my day," she said. "You should, too. It's a painless way to up your activity level."

"Can I stay in the car?"

Mrs. Dagnitz sighed loudly. "I love you, Minnow."

"Love you, too." I looked out the window at a bum in a dirty hot-pink parka trundling by with a shopping cart full of empty bottles. It was so hot, how could he wear that parka?

Mrs. Dagnitz hopped out of the car without another word. I watched her narrow back as she marched away from the car, and then I called Angus Paine.

- 2 -

Mrs. Dagnitz dropped me off in front of Casa Clark after telling me three times to put the groceries away. Compared with the other pretty, wood-shingled houses on our street, our big stucco box looks like a Mexican restaurant. Quills, my brother who is the bassist for the band Humongous Bag of Cashews, says it is something called "eclectic," a fancy word for "freakish."

I grabbed the plastic bag full of groceries, hauled myself out of the car, and slammed the door a teeny bit harder than was necessary. Mrs. Dagnitz watched me from over her sunglasses. She didn't say another word about "working it." Just the thought of that conversation practically gave me a seizure, which is how I always feel when I'm too embarrassed to even speak. Mrs. Dagnitz roared off to pick up Mr. Dagnitz from yoga. Why they couldn't leave their yoga back in Santa Fe, I don't know.

When I saw Kevin's blue bike propped against the side of the house, I got a funny feeling in my chest, as if a helium balloon were stuck in there. It was such a relief to come home and see that dumb little BMX bike. Kevin was going into ninth grade and had a real summer job. He worked as a manny, a man-nanny, and spent his days playing Legos and opening juice boxes for Harvey and Otis, a pair of eight-year-old boys who belonged to his mom's coworker. Kevin made ten dollars an hour. In my humble opinion that is a lot of money for a ninth grader.

I dropped the bag of groceries on the kitchen counter and tossed the halibut into the fridge. Last year in health we'd learned that leaving fish out on the counter could kill you. I'd put the other stuff away later. I figured I had a half hour until Mrs. Dagnitz returned.

From upstairs, I could hear Xbox sounds of cartoon bad guys getting blown up. I took the stairs two at a time. I was less happy to see Kevin when I found him in the TV room playing a video game with Morgan, my youngest older brother. Even though Kevin had been my official boyfriend for less than two weeks, I suspected that he came over to see my brothers as much as to see me. Kevin had a snotty older sister but no brothers. I have no sisters and three brothers, and it is more or less Boy Central around my house all the time. Which is part of why it was a little strange having Mrs. Dagnitz flitting in and out. Luckily, she was not staying at Casa Clark with Mr. Dagnitz. Even though my dad, Charlie, was out of town on lawyer business until the end of the month, it would still feel bizarre waking up in the morning and seeing them sitting at the table drinking their coffee.

Kevin and Morgan were perched on the edge of Cat Pee Couch, so named because we once had an evil tabby cat that sprayed the legs of whoever sat in her spot. That tabby is long gone and the couch has been drenched with an expensive pet-odor remover, but on hot summer days you can sometimes still catch a whiff of that bad old cat. Kevin wore khaki shorts and a blue striped polo shirt. He was six feet tall, with shiny brown-blond hair and mountain-lake-blue eyes. I was pretty sure I would marry Kevin one day when we were thirty and he had gotten his PhD in marine biology and had saved the world's coral reefs and I had gotten tired of my life as a globe-trotting sleuth solving important mysteries they normally reserved for Scotland Yard and places like that. Only then would we be ready to buy our ranch on the island of Maui, where we would surf and raise Appaloosas. I wasn't quite sure what those were, but Kevin assured me they were most excellent.

Morgan wore his trademark earflap hat, even though it was the dead middle of a humid Portland summer.

It was almost never hot in our city, but when the heat finally showed up, it became the guest that wouldn't leave. Even in the middle of the night it could be eighty-five degrees. People said that's because we live in a valley, something to do with the hot air getting stuck.

Ned slept curled between them, snoring into his paws. The room was stuffy and smelled of clean dog—Ned had just had a bath—cheese pizza, and chlorine. Kevin was a champion swimmer, which meant he always smelled of chlorine. He swam the butterfly, the most show-offy stroke there is.

"Hey," I said.

"Hey," said Morgan, glancing up at me.

"I can't believe you still have that hat on. It's eight hundred degrees in here," I said. Between the boys and the dog, there was nowhere for me to sit.

"It's my good-luck hat," said Morgan.

"Hey, babe," said Kevin. I liked how he called me babe, even though it sort of sounded like something he'd practiced at home in the mirror, winking and pointing at himself with finger guns.

"You can't hide from me, suckah!" Kevin's thumbs jigged around the controller as he blasted away. On the screen, the cartoon bad guys threw up their hands and screamed before they exploded. I stood in the doorway for a long minute. He never looked away from the screen.

I'll tell you one thing: I'm never going to be one of

those girls who watches her boyfriend play video games and calls that hanging out. It is more boring than weeding the yard. It is more boring than a parental lecture. It is even more boring than when boys *talk* about playing video games. How is that possible?

I turned around and ran up the stairs to my bedroom on the third floor.

My ferret, Jupiter, used to sleep in a cage behind the grand piano in the living room downstairs, but after Ned arrived, we bought him a fancy new ferret tower, with four levels connected by ramps and tubes, and moved him to my bedroom. Ned liked to stand in front of Jupiter's cage, madly wagging his stump of a tail. We couldn't tell if that meant he wanted Jupiter to be his friend or his snack.

I opened Jupiter's cage, scooped him up from where he was conked out in his hammock, and tossed him onto my bed. Jupiter doesn't mind being airborne. He throws his little white legs out wide like a flying squirrel. As usual, he behaved as if he'd never been out of his cage until that very second. He performed his mad inchworm dance until he fell off the bed, bumped into a chair leg, pulled one of my flip-flops under the bed, scampered back out and attacked a wadded-up piece of paper, hurled himself into the air for no good reason, fell backward, dove into one of my shoes, and then was distracted by a CD that had fallen on the floor and that he tried to drag under my dresser.

I plopped down on my bed and watched Jupiter for a while. I crossed my legs and thought about my second conversation with Angus Paine. I'd waited until Mrs. Dagnitz had walked all the way across the supermarket parking lot and disappeared into the market before calling him back. It was too easy. I just had to hit the button that dialed the number of the last incoming call. Tip tap, just like that, and the strange boy was on the line.

I told him I'd love to help him figure out who had burned down his family's grocery store.

"All right," he said. He sounded distant, much less warm and friendly than when he'd called me only the hour before. He was annoyed, distracted. I'd say he was playing video games, but I couldn't hear any noise in the background.

"When do you want to meet?" I said.

Pause.

"Whatever works for you," he said.

"Are you still there? Hello?" I said loudly. I knew he hadn't hung up, but his behavior truly bugged. Hadn't *he* called *me*?

"Let's make it two o'clock tomorrow then," he said. "At the grocery."

Is it considered hanging up on somebody if you don't say good-bye? If it is, then Angus Paine had hung up on me. As I snapped my phone shut, I realized I hadn't asked for directions to Corbett Street

Grocery. But then again, he hadn't offered to give me the address either. Did he think that just because his family's grocery was on Cryptkeeper Ron's Tour of Haunted Portland that I would automatically know where it was? Or maybe between the time Angus Paine first called me and the time I'd called him back, he'd found someone else to help him. Or maybe he'd just decided to forget it.

Man, was it hot up there. The windows were wide open over my desk, but the air was dead still, a breeze the last thing on its sluggish mind. I pulled my hair up and tied it in a knot on top of my head, tugged off my khaki pants, kicked them into the back of my closet, and put on some jean shorts. I have a theory that the reason why jeans never go out of style is that you can fish them out of a dirty clothes pile and they are never wrinkled. They can pass for clean longer than any other type of clothing.

I was just about to settle in with my rebus notebook when I heard someone clomping up the stairs to the third floor.

Kevin!

. . . who was not supposed to be in my bedroom at all, ever.

The second day Kevin was my boyfriend Mark Clark came home from work early and caught us smooching in the TV room. My face was so red I thought I might give myself sunburn. Kevin leaped up when Mark appeared in the doorway, then got one look at the paid-assassin expression on my brother's face and made up an excuse about having to go home for dinner, even though he was supposed to be having dinner with us.

After Kevin left, Mark Clark demanded to know if our mom had ever talked to me about the birds and the bees. The birds and the bees! Does anyone under the age of ninety even call it that anymore? I could not believe we were having this conversation. From the look on Mark Clark's face, he could not believe we were having it either. Mark Clark was sweating, giant pit stains beneath his arms.

We'd been standing in the kitchen. For some reason I was holding a can of refried beans. I was so traumatized, I cannot remember why I was holding a can of refried beans. I told him I needed to practice the piano and ran into the living room and started pounding on our baby grand. I haven't taken piano lessons in five years. Then Mark Clark came after me and said I wasn't allowed to have Kevin in my room. Never *ever* EVER. A week later, I found the can of beans under the piano bench.

Now Kevin came over and sat on the other edge of my bed. There was nothing weird about it. Why Mark Clark was so hysterical, I don't know. Kevin turned my rebus notebook toward him and took a mechanical pencil out of his pocket. Kevin is the kind of boy who always has a mechanical pencil (but not a pocket protector). He wrote:

S
B
A
R
G

"That would be 'Stand up for sbarg,'" I said.

"Ha ha," said Kevin. "Too easy, huh?"

"Up for grabs," I said. "I think I already did that one."

"I just made it up," he said.

"You probably stole it from me," I said. I reached over and poked him in his side. He waggled his eyebrows at me. A smooch was most definitely incoming. At the same time, I heard a car door slam outside in the driveway, beneath my window.

It was Mark Clark! It was Mrs. Dagnitz! It was some authority figure capable of getting me GOT—Grounded Off Technology—which meant no television, DVD player, computer, or cell phone. It was the equivalent of being flung back into the Stone Age, and should have been illegal, like selling children into slavery.

I hopped off the bed, trying to be casual instead of hysterical. I could still see Mark Clark saying, "Never *ever* EVER!" This must be evidence that I'm not boy crazy, because I would much rather pass up a smooch from Kevin than get grounded for the rest of the summer.

"Heyyyy. Come back here," Kevin said.

"Incoming ferret," I said. I reached down and scooped up Jupiter from where he was hauling one of my Chuck Taylors around by the shoestring. I tossed him into Kevin's lap.

"Today some dude called me about solving an arson," I said.

"I thought we were chillaxing here," said Kevin. More eyebrow waggling. He patted the place on my bed where I had just been sitting. Kevin had very dark eyebrows compared with his hair. He said it was because his family was Black Irish. I don't know what that is. Note to self: Google "Black Irish."

Pat pat pat. "Come here, babe."

"Someone burned down his family's grocery store," I said.

Kevin sighed. I could tell he realized there was going to be no rolling around on my bed today. "They say arson is the toughest crime to solve. I saw a show on it on the Discovery Channel."

"Tougher than murder?" I asked. I had already solved a murder.

"The evidence is usually destroyed by the fire. What started the fire gets burned up in it. Wicked sketchy, huh?" he said.

"You mean—"

"Let's say you use a rag drenched in gasoline to start a fire. What's the first thing that gets burned to a crisp? The rag. So the cops come in, have a look around, can't find any physical evidence, and close the case. Now come back over here."

"I don't think you're supposed to be up here," I said. "My brother might come after you with his dojo."

Kevin laughed. "Isn't there where you go to take karate lessons?"

I didn't know. Mojo? Hojo? I thought a dojo was one of those weapons boys always think are so cool.

From downstairs I could hear voices and cupboard doors slamming.

"Uh-oh. The groceries."

I dashed out of my room, tore to the end of hallway, hopped onto the fireman's pole, and slid down into the kitchen. Luckily I'd put lotion on my legs that morning. The fireman's pole was here when we moved in—don't ask me why the family who lived in this house before us thought they needed one. The advantage of the fireman's pole was that you dropped into the kitchen like a ninja. I hardly ever used it, but once in a while it was one hundred percent handy.

I expected to see Mrs. Dagnitz putting away the groceries with her back mad-mom straight and her mouth a thin-lipped line of pure rage, but instead, there was Weird Rolando, my mom's new husband, folding the plastic grocery bag and tucking it into the recycling bin. He wore his brown-and-gray hair in a braid. My mother is married to a man whose hair is longer than mine. That should be against the law.

"Sorry about the groceries," I said to his back. "I told Mrs. Dag . . . I told my mom I'd put them away, then I sort of spaced it."

"It happens," said Weird Rolando. He turned around and flashed me a smile. It was real, not one of those fake ones where the mouth does all the work. I would never tell my brothers this, but I don't mind Weird Rolando. He is the sort of person to take home a lost dog and then make up flyers saying he'd found it. Once upon a time, not long after my mom and dad separated, Rolando was my mother's yoga teacher. My mother lost weight, got very good at standing on her head, then announced she was moving to Santa Fe, and away she went. "It's not a big deal," he said.

"It is a big deal when I specifically asked you to put them away not ten minutes ago," said Mrs. Dagnitz, hurrying into the kitchen from the dining room, flinging open the refrigerator, and grabbing the same spinach Rolando had put away seven seconds earlier.

"Sorry," I said. "I did put the fish away. Isn't that the important one?" I didn't think it would help to make up some excuse. Mrs. Dagnitz had that deep wrinkle between her eyebrows. I remembered how it was with that wrinkle—once it showed up, there was nothing you could do about it. Like with the stomach flu, you just had to wait until it went away.

"Clearly you haven't heard about what's going on with spinach," she snapped. "E.coli and God knows what else."

"I thought that was from not washing it."

"Are you trying to kill us?"

"My plot is revealed," I said.

Out of the corner of my eye I thought I saw Weird Rolando, *my stepfather*, smile. He started rubbing Mrs. Dagnitz's shoulders. She rolled her neck around, this way and that. "I'm just so stressed out over this reception," she said.

"It'll be fine, Buttercup," said Weird Rolando.

"We should have splurged for the shrimp," she said. "It's the perfect wedding reception nibble. People love shrimp at a wedding reception, don't they? It's festive, shrimp is. And so pretty."

"Just breathe, Buttercup," said Rolando, and he continued pressing his thumbs into her back.

Buttercup. I looked all around the kitchen—at the bright orange counters that Mrs. Dagnitz had always complained about but that no one else seemed to notice, at the Great Chili Peppers of the World poster hung next to the fridge, at the back door, next to which sat two blue recycling bins, at anything, anything but the two of them. *Buttercup*. Could they see me cringe? Did they even care?

From upstairs, I could hear thumping around. I hoped Kevin was still watching Jupiter, but I bet he'd drifted back down to the TV room. That was all right. I'd rather have him hypnotized by a video game, safely upstairs with Morgan, than in the kitchen having to hear *my stepfather* call my mother *Buttercup*.

I wished I was meeting Angus Paine that very minute. I was getting used to having a mystery to solve. It distracted me from a lot of things, like Mr. and Mrs. Dagnitz standing in the middle of the kitchen, with their eyes closed, breathing loudly.

Eventually Mrs. Dagnitz got over being stressed about the shrimp and started cleaning the spinach. "I could use a little help here," she said, shaking the water off one small leaf and setting it on a piece of paper towel. Whenever Mrs. Dagnitz was around, we always had spinach salad instead of regular lettuce salad because, according to Mrs. Dagnitz, lettuce was not a real vegetable but only crunchy water.

I went to the sink and tore a spinach leaf from its stalk. It felt limp and gritty.

"No no no," she said impatiently. "I need you to chop the mushrooms."

Let me re-introduce myself—Minerva Clark, mind reader. Mrs. Dagnitz was like this. All supernice, buying me clothes no matter the cost, and necklaces I didn't need, then acting all harsh. I knew I was in the moody freak stage of life, but what was her problem? I know what my brothers say it is: guilt, pure and simple. I retrieved the plastic bag of mushrooms from the fridge.

"And we're having the fish, too?" I asked, just to have something to say. I promised myself that if I was ever a mother, I would never be so awful that my kid was forced to make conversation about halibut.

Weird Rolando drifted into the dining room to work on his jigsaw puzzle. He was a jigsaw-puzzle freak. He liked the ones that drove you insane—a huge pile of similar-colored marbles, a close-up of a colored pencil, fish scales.

As we worked, Mrs. Dagnitz got over my leaving the nonperishable groceries out for ten minutes. She said, "Tomorrow afternoon we need to get you some shoes."

"Okay," I said. The second the word was out of my mouth I remembered that I was meeting Angus Paine at two o'clock. "I'm supposed to meet Chelsea at two o'clock. Do you remember my friend Chelsea? The one with the really cute clothes all the time?"

"The well-groomed one?" asked Mrs. Dagnitz.

"With the nice, straight, shiny hair," I said. In Mrs. Dagnitz's book, having nice, straight, shiny hair was the sure sign that you were a superior person in all ways.

"Well, we need to get you some shoes," said Mrs. Dagnitz. "I haven't seen what's in your closet, but I'm sure you've got nothing suitable."

"When I get home maybe? We're just hanging out at her house. She has some hair products she wants to show me, and we want to burn some CDs, and maybe we'll go to the mall and people-watch." What was I saying? Why was I going on and on? Lying was bad enough. But it seemed to make my mother feel better that I had a friend who knew about the joy of living in the world of shoes.

Mrs. Dagnitz didn't say anything else about shopping. She chopped the red onion and kept saying "damn it" as she wiped away her tears with the pinky finger of each hand, daintily.

"There's a skin-diving mask under the sink. Mark Clark uses it when he chops onions and he never cries."

She stopped chopping and looked at me. "A skin-diving mask?"

"It works," I said.

"This family is so strange," she said.

This family *is* so strange.

Whenever Mrs. Dagnitz is around, time slows to half its normal speed. She put the fish in the oven, then performed her evening yoga exercises in the backyard. Kevin came downstairs and said he needed to head on home. His cousins were coming over, and they had tickets to a baseball game. He got a drink of water at the sink. Together we watched Mrs. Dagnitz bend over and lift one of her legs high in the air. I am a bad person. I chose that moment to let the dog Ned outside. He scampered over to Mrs. Dagnitz, barking and leaping in the air and nipping at Mrs. Dagnitz's heel until she was forced to chase him around the yard. Kevin left without trying for another smooch. I waved at his back as he sped off down the driveway on his bike. Just as I thought he wasn't going to turn around, he did. He grinned and waved and almost ran into a parked car. I got the helium-balloon-in-my-chest feeling all over again. Kevin had just gotten his braces off. He has the nicest teeth.

– 3 –

It took almost an hour to get to Corbett Street Grocery by bus, which gave me plenty of time to wish I hadn't told Mrs. Dagnitz I was hanging out with Chelsea de Guzman today. After we'd solved the mystery of what happened to the red diamond belonging to her father, Louis de Guzman, Chelsea had been my best friend for forty-eight hours. Then, over the last week, Chelsea had become best friends with Hannah, who used to be my best friend, long ago, last year. Chelsea changed best friends more often than most people floss their teeth. Chelsea hadn't answered any of my text messages in more than a week. One day I was moping around and Quills asked me what was wrong. I told him and he said girls my age were evil incarnate. I'm not sure what "incarnate" means, exactly. I bet girls who lie to their moms are also evil incarnate.

Corbett Street was shady and lined with narrow two-story houses. Some were painted purple and pink and had crazy lawn ornaments and gardens overgrown with roses and sunflowers. Some of the houses had those Tibetan prayer flags strung across their sagging front porches. People had small gardens between their houses. A CD was playing somewhere—or it may even have been a vinyl record—one of those old seventies man singers with a high bleating voice. Corbett Street was a street of old hippies.

I'd never seen a real live burned-down building before. On the phone Angus Paine had said there was only one wall left standing. But Corbett Street Grocery didn't look burned down to me at all. It sat on the street's only sunny corner. There was a mural on the side—an erupting volcano shooting out not lava but wholesome food. The volcano had snow on it, and there were pine trees in the background. The biggest tomatoes and zucchinis you've ever seen in your life were spewing out of that snowy volcano. This looked like a lot more than one wall to me. I wondered if there'd even been a fire. Then I walked around to the front of the grocery and it was a different story.

The door looked as if a giant had borrowed it for a bonfire, then put it back on the hinges. It was as black as black could be, shiny with tiny cracks. The address numerals—222—were made of some metal that hadn't burned but gave off a weird rainbow sheen. The windows on the second floor above the door were all broken. The black smears above the windows looked as if they had been made with the side of a charcoal stick (the most difficult art media to work with, according to our art teacher, Ms. Schulte-Vincente).

I peeked inside the plate-glass window. It was pure disaster, nothing but big piles of unrecognizable rubble. Strips of ceiling hung down. Paint curled away from the wall. The only thing that didn't look blistered or burned was a sink and a tall metal shelf that jutted out into the middle of the room. This must have been the wall Angus Paine was talking about.

Oooo-oooo-oooo-ahhnn! Thumpa-thumpa-thumpa. *Oooo-oooo-oooo-ahhnn!* Thumpa-thumpa-thumpa. My cell phone. I fished it out of my back pocket.

Before I could say hello, a voice said, "You're way better looking than your picture in the newspaper." It was Angus Paine, being a total flirt monster. This was nothing like what he'd been like before on the phone. And they said that girls were total schizos.

"I could have told you *that*," I said. "I'm at the grocery. Where are you?"

"Behind you," he said.

I spun around to see a boy about my height wearing a black trench coat, cell phone pressed to his ear, striding across the street. I try not to judge people by their clothes, but a boy in a black trench coat in the middle of summer means one thing only: tragic gamer who's convinced deep down that he's a vampire, even though he won't admit it. Angus Paine had dark copper-colored hair and a million dark brown freckles. He had stubble on his jaw. Stubble. I didn't think he was any older than me, and he already shaved.

We stared at each other. His eyes were dark brown. He even had a few freckles on his eyelids. I am the queen of staredowns, but Angus Paine just kept looking at me. Maybe he wasn't a flirt monster at all, but a total nutcase. Finally, he released a lopsided grin and asked me if I wanted a Starburst. His big front tooth had a chip out of it that shouted skateboarding accident.

"Starbursts are my all-time favorite candy," I said.

"I know," he said. "It was in the paper." He groped around in the pocket of his trench coat and pulled out a package of Tropical Chews.

"Oh, right." I'd read the story about seven times, but I'd forgotten how the reporter said I loved Starbursts.

"I'm a Mango Melon man myself," he said, unwrapping one and popping it into his mouth. Angus Paine even had freckles on his lips. "Did you see the damage?" he asked.

Together we pressed our noses against the plate-glass window. I sniffed. Angus Paine was wearing cologne or aftershave. It was Old Spice, the same stuff Mark Clark put on too much of before he went out with someone he really liked. O-kaay. What was that about?

"I thought you said there was only one wall left standing," I said.

"Yeah well, I exaggerated." He laughed. He reached over and gave me a slow-motion punch in the arm. "The toaster collection's still there, though. That's a good thing."

"Toaster collection?"

"On top of that metal shelf. Moms has the biggest old-toaster collection in America. See?" He tapped the glass with his finger. The shelf was at the back of the store, near the walk-in freezer. It was dim near the back of the store. I could just make out a row of square shapes along the top of the shelf.

"In the entire country?"

"Nah," he said. "But it's pretty big."

He reached again into the pocket of his trench coat and pulled out a key. It seemed odd to me that it wasn't on a key chain. The burned front door was locked with a shiny silver hasp and padlock.

Inside, the grocery smelled like a campfire. I remembered Angus telling me about his Grams, who had died in the apartment upstairs. I breathed through my mouth; I didn't want to smell anything *at all* that reminded me of what happened to her. I tried not to think about it. I tried to be interested in the piles of debris. On top of one of them was a half-burned box of Lucky Charms. In the back of the grocery, I saw where the entire ceiling had collapsed.

Now that I was here, I remembered it from Cryptkeeper Ron's Tour of Haunted Portland. Cryptkeeper Ron was a local weirdo my dad's age who owned a bunch of auto dealerships and was always running for mayor. He broke out his Tour of Haunted Portland every Halloween, advertising like mad on cheesy cable stations.

As I walked around, I realized I didn't know the first thing about finding an arsonist. I thought about what Kevin had said, that fire consumes its own evidence. Why did that sound so creepy?

"How did you say the fire started?" I asked.

"Didn't," said Angus Paine. "The investigators are saying the gas main broke sometime during the night and the grocery store filled up with gas—then when the electric motor for the world-famous walk-in freezer kicked in, the gas caught fire. The freezer and the gas line are, like, ancient. Of course, I have my own ideas."

I turned and looked at him standing by the door, his hands thrust deep in his trench-coat pockets. He'd been checking me check out the damage. There was something about the tone of his voice. He was lying. Or something.

I opened one of the freezer's thick glass doors. Cans of soda and plastic bottles of sports drinks sat in their neat rows. This is where the ghost was supposed to live. Even though the electricity hadn't been on since the fire, the air inside was cold.

"So does the ghost still live here?" I asked.

"*Kikimora*. She's a Kikimora. We don't know."

"She has a name?" I asked.

"Her name is actually Louise," he said. "I thought they mentioned that on the tour. A Kikimora is a type of ghost, an entity that inhabits a house and is usually pretty happy and helpful unless someone tries to get rid of her."

"Huh," I said.

"You think I'm a dork," Angus said suddenly.

At that moment, a man appeared in the doorway. He carried a clipboard. The light was behind him, so I couldn't see the expression on his face. He was shorter than me, dressed all businessman in a suit and tie, even though it had to have been about a hundred degrees out.

"What's going on here?" he said. His voice was the deep voice of a boss, but it was flat, sort of robotic sounding.

"Deputy Chief Huntington! How are you this fine day?" Angus stuck his hand out for a big grown-up handshake. He released his lopsided grin, phony polite. "This is my good friend Minerva. She's into fires. Interested in fires, I mean. I was just showing her what happened."

"Interested in fires?" said Chief Huntington.

"Well, you know," said Angus. "She likes fire. I mean, likes looking at fires! At the damage fires do, I mean." He hit himself on the side of the head, as if he were trying to knock the goofiness out.

"I don't, actually," said Deputy Chief Huntington. "Your folks know you're poking around here?"

"Come on, Minerva," said Angus suddenly. He stalked out without answering, his trench coat billowing behind him, Zorro-like, geeky but dramatic.

"Are you investigating the arson?" I asked Deputy Chief Huntington. I think he had a glass eye or a dead eye or something, because one eye looked at you hard, as if he were performing an X-ray, and the other seemed to be staring off over your shoulder.

"Why do you think it was arson?" He looked at me with his one X-ray eye. Since he was just my height, his ears were eye level. They were the largest ears I think I'd ever seen.

"Angus said it was," I said, feeling suddenly as if I didn't have the entire story. "It's not?"

"An accident, the best we can tell," said the deputy chief. He stood beneath the hole in the ceiling, poked at something in the wall with his pen, and jotted some notes on his clipboard. "Just double-checking a few things, then we're signing off on it. We have no reason to think it's arson." He made another note, then looked at me as if he thought I was lying about something. "Do we?"

I found Angus a block away, sitting on the curb eating an egg-salad sandwich. The other half of the sandwich sat beside him in its plastic triangle.

"Robotective back there gives me the creeps," he said. "Have a seat."

"What's the deal?" I said. "I thought you said it was arson. The deputy chief says it was an accident."

"Did you notice his voice? He sounds like Hal from *2001: A Space Odyssey*. You ever see *2001: A Space Odyssey*? Awesome flick."

"I like the eye."

"Robotective's Eye of Doom?"

I laughed, even though we were entering the realm of making fun of somebody with a disability. Not cool.

"Of course Robotective wants to rule it an accident. That way, the cops don't have to do any work. Just sign a few forms, and it's back to sitting at their desks eating doughnuts and surfing the Net. I wish it was that easy for my family."

"What do you mean? There's probably insurance or something that'll pay for the damage."

"Insurance?" He snorted.

"Property insurance or something," I said. I stuck my hands in my pockets and felt the heft of my phone. Why was he in such a moody freak mood? Across the street two little girls hobbled past, each one wearing an inline skate on one foot and a flip-flop on the other.

"My parents spend every single day arguing with the insurance people," said Angus. "They won't pay out if it's an old gas line that should have been replaced a long time ago. That's our fault, they say." He took a huge angry bite of his sandwich and chewed it in a way that reminded me of Ned the dog tearing into one of his rawhide bones. "At least if it gets ruled arson, my family gets some money to rebuild. That store is all my parents have. Plus, my mom just had hip-replacement surgery. It's sucky all around."

"Maybe it *was* an accident," I said.

"This half is for you," he said. He balanced the plastic triangle holding the other half of the egg-salad sandwich on my knee, then reached into his trench-coat pocket and pulled out a cream soda.

"Aren't you hot in that trench coat?" I asked.

"It wasn't an accident," he went on.

"Well, who would have a reason to burn it down? You said your grandma lived above the store—"

"Grams wasn't *my* grandmother." He said it in a way that said I was an idiot for thinking such a thing.

"But you said—"

"Grams is what we all called her. Nat and Nat call her Grams. She was really Wade's grandma. He lived up there, too. Nat and Nat are my parents. Just so you know. Natalie and Nathan. Such an adorable couple."

"Why are you being so emo all of a sudden? I'm just trying to help. Jeez."

He turned and looked at me with his almost black eyes. His face was close. I could smell his Old Spice and the mayonnaise from the egg salad, which it suddenly occurred to me we should not be eating in such killer heat. I put my half back in the container.

"Sorry. I'm just a little stressed. I grew up in this store," he said, all sad-dog-looking.

"I get that," I said. "It's just that I'm not sure how I can help you. I mean, Robotective in there is about to rule it an accident. Maybe it was an accident. Maybe you just don't want to face that your parents, you know, *should* have replaced the gas pipes, or whatever. Maybe there's no mystery here." As soon as I said that, I understood that I didn't want it to be true. I wanted a mystery. I needed a mystery. I had become a mystery-o-holic.

"Oh, there's a mystery," he said. "There's always a mystery."

If I hadn't known better, I would have thought Angus Paine was going to lean over and give me a smooch, right there, sitting on the curb smack in the middle of the day, with the sun baking the parts in our hair and the occasional car tootling past and Deputy Detective Chief Inspector Whatever inside Angus's family's store making notes on his clipboard and . . . and . . .

Oooo-oooo-oooo-ahhnn! Thumpa-thumpa-thumpa. *Oooo-oooo-oooo-ahhnn!* Thumpa-thumpa-thumpa.

My phone! I jumped, knocking my half of egg-salad sandwich into the gutter and kicking Angus in the leg at the same time.

Angus laughed. "Nice ring tone." He reached down and untied my shoelace. Flirt monster.

"I got it from my friend Reggie, who got it from

someone who works at some famous zoo. It's not just any gorilla, it's a gorilla in the wild, and she's a she, not a he." I flipped open the phone. Why was I nattering away like this? I was no stranger to dealing with flirt monsters! Well, all right, actually I was. The only true flirt monster I'd ever come into contact with was Kevin, who was now my boyfriend, whom I would probably marry in seventeen years.

It was Mark Clark. "Where ARE you?" The annoyance in his voice practically leaped out and bit me on the nose. The instant I heard his voice, I remembered that I was supposed to be home. I told him I was on my way. I spared him a lame excuse. Mark Clark was the kind of person who would let you mess up once in a while without wondering whether it would be better off for everyone if you were sent to a teen boot camp.

"Mom's waiting," said Mark Clark. "You know how she gets when she thinks she's going to be late. She's already starting to rearrange the furniture."

"Tell her I'll be there in a minute," I said.

"Would that make me a liar?" said Mark Clark. "Because that's all I need, Minerva." He sighed so loudly it hurt my ear. Life hadn't been easy for Mark Clark lately. Normally Mark Clark was in charge, which meant he got to make up the rules. Then Mrs. Dagnitz showed up out of nowhere, and her rules won out over Mark Clark's rules, but Mark Clark was still somehow in charge.

"I'm on my way," I said. I leaped to my feet and started powering my way back down Corbett Street toward the bus stop. Angus caught up with me easily, his black trench coat flapping out behind him. He strode beside me, as if I'd invited him along.

"So it shouldn't take you longer than ten?" Mark Clark asked. "Where are you, Chelsea's?"

"What?" I said loudly. "You're breaking up. See you in a few minutes." I snapped the phone shut.

"I'm late for a doctor's appointment," I said to Angus, who bopped along beside me, his lopsided grin permanently plastered on his freckled face. It seemed as if he'd forgotten all about the arson.

"Really?" he said. "You look very healthy to me."

We hurried past the grocery store. Robotective Huntington stood in the burned-out doorway writing something on his clipboard. His eye stared at us over the top of a pair of reading glasses. His gaze shifted to me, where it stuck too long. I'm sure it wasn't my imagination. He was wondering about me, somehow.

I felt my head start to sweat. How could I have lost track of the time? What was Robotective Huntington staring at? And what about the grocery? Was it arson or not?

"What's wrong with you?" Angus persisted.

"I was supposed to be home right now. And my mom goes totally insane if somebody makes her late. She thinks people do it to her on purpose, just to see her go crazy. It's times like these I am so glad she doesn't live with us anymore."

"No, I mean what's wrong that you're going to the doctor?"

"It's the brain doctor."

"Just a checkup then?" he asked.

"You're awfully nosy," I said. We'd reached the bus stop. Of course, there was no bus in sight. I sighed and checked the time on my cell phone.

"You're not taking the bus, are you?"

"How'd you think I got here? Unlike you, I didn't just materialize from a mist."

"Materialize from a mist?" Angus's voice flew up like every other boy I knew. I guess that meant he wasn't a four-hundred-year-old vampire after all.

"Aren't you hot in that trench coat?" I asked again. Angus was starting to get on my nerves. I pulled out my phone and checked the time again. I was so dead. I was so not going to be home in a few minutes.

"Why don't you take my scooter?" Angus said. His brown-black eyes snapped with something I couldn't read. For no reason on earth, he patted me on the head.

Angus's Go-Ped had an orange-and-black deck and an electric motor in the back. It looked like a regular scooter, but you didn't need to push it to make it go. It went eighteen miles an hour and got me home in about ten minutes, the wind whipping my mass of bed-head hair around behind me. The breeze felt so good. Never had I looked like such a geek, riding the streets of Portland in my turquoise Chuck Taylor high-tops and jean skirt. Lucky for me, Portland is the alternative-transportation capital of the nation—aside from all the bicycles and mopeds, there's a guy in our neighborhood who has a pair of miniature horses that pull him around in a cart. No one bats an eye.

– 4 –

Even though I was now a one-of-a-kind freak with uncommon self-esteem, I was not immune to total stupidity. I was so desperate to get home, I had borrowed Angus's Go-Ped without stopping to think how I would explain it. I could say I borrowed it from Chelsea, but there was not a drop of pink or purple anywhere on it, so no one would believe me. Plus, I'd already lied enough for one day. My brother Morgan was a Buddhist and said lying ruined your karma. I hoped karma ran along the same principles as tooth decay—it took a lot more than one Tropical Starburst to ruin your teeth. My plan was to zoom up the driveway and straight into the garage, in the hopes no one would see me. I'd figure out how to get the scooter back to Angus later.

But when I finally reached our house, Mark Clark and Mrs. Dagnitz were standing in the middle of the driveway, waiting beside Mrs. Dagnitz's white SUV. Even though it was brain-cooking hot outside. Even though they were both wearing slacks. If they were surprised to see me speed up on an electric scooter, they didn't let on. Mark Clark had the straight-lipped, big-eyed look he gets when something has disturbed his world. Mrs. Dagnitz, on the other hand, was smiling the biggest tooth-whitened smile you can imagine. I had not seen such an enormous life-affirming smile since the first day of kindergarten, when our teacher, Mrs. Yerby, who also rescued cats with terminal diseases, welcomed us to our new school.

I smiled back. I thought it would be good to pretend that Mrs. Dagnitz's fake smile was a real smile. "Hey there!" I hopped off the scooter as if I'd owned it for years. Maybe Mrs. Dagnitz would think Charlie, our dad and her ex-husband, had given it to me to make me feel better because my own mother had deserted me for a guy who thought dressing up meant wearing black yoga pants.

Right.

"Why look, if it isn't Minerva Clark. How nice of you to interrupt your busy schedule and join us," cried Mrs. Dagnitz. She was also wearing a peach-colored cotton sweater tied around her shoulders. Pastels were Mrs. Dagnitz's black.

"Sorry," I mumbled to Mark Clark. "I lost track of the time."

"Better get in the car," he said under his breath.

I couldn't get in until I did something with the scooter. Mark Clark said we could throw it in the back of the Pathfinder. He didn't ask where I got it. Mrs. Dagnitz didn't ask where I got it. This was not good. The mad-at-Minerva vibes were so powerful, I thought they might ignite the gas tank. I thought someone's hair might catch on fire. I moved to open the back door, and Mrs. Dagnitz, who was already sitting in the driver's seat, rolled down the window. "Oh, no no no. Sit in the front with me!"

I slowly walked around the back of the car, hoping I would get points in heaven, or somewhere, for remembering not to walk in front of the car.

"So!" Mrs. Dagnitz cried as we roared off down the street. "Did you have fun at Chelsea's house?"

I took a deep cleansing breath like Mrs. Dagnitz urges me to do every other minute and waited. I looked straight ahead through the windshield. I messed with the air-conditioning knobs and switches; it was as hot as an equatorial nation. I waited some more.

Mrs. Dagnitz had been away in New Mexico too long. She thought I was still eleven years old. She didn't realize I'd gotten clever. I'd caught on to her old trick. She didn't give a rip about Chelsea, or what I'd done over at Chelsea's. She was hoping I would think I'd gotten away with it, and having gotten away with it, would make up more stuff just because I thought it was safe.

"Did you talk about boys and paint each other's

toenails and sing into the end of your hairbrush in front of the mirror?"

"The end of my hairbrush?" Somewhere between yesterday and today my mother had gone mental. I spun around and looked at Mark Clark, sitting behind me in the backseat. He gave a shrug and looked out the window. We sped over the Broadway bridge. The metal grating went *thonka-thonka-thonka* as our car rolled over it.

"Don't look at him!" said Mrs. Dagnitz.

"Mom, take it easy," said Mark Clark.

"I never sing into the end of my hairbrush," I said. "I prefer the saltshaker, that wooden one you and Dad got—"

Mrs. Dagnitz reached over and slapped my thigh—hard.

Mrs. Dagnitz may be slightly insane, but she is not a child abuser. The only time she's ever laid a hand on me was when I was three and she smacked me on the arm with an empty box of Froot Loops because I tipped my cereal bowl over at the breakfast table.

"Stop it!" she said.

"Ow!" I said, even though it didn't hurt. I was surprised more than anything.

"Hey, hey, hey," said Mark Clark.

"Your little friend Chelsea called the house!" said Mrs. Dagnitz. "Now, why on earth would she have called our house if you were over at her house?"

"She called on the land line?" I was incredulous. Why didn't she call me on my cell?

"Do not change the subject, Minerva. Where were you? With that boyfriend? With that Kevin person?"

"Uh, nooooo . . . I was not with Kevin." I said it in a way that made it sound as if I were lying.

"Do you think I was born yesterday?" said Mrs. Dagnitz. "I had a boyfriend when I was your age. I know how it is. I do not want you hanging out with him when there are no parents around."

"How do you even know there were no parents around?"

Mrs. Dagnitz fiddled with the rearview mirror so she could glare at Mark Clark while she drove. I didn't think that was very safe. In two and a half years when I get my permit, I'm sure that I will never be allowed to adjust the rearview mirror so I can have a conversation with someone in the backseat while I am driving.

"Is she always like this?"

"Worse," said Mark Clark. "She used to have a meth lab, right in the basement."

"Don't you start, too!" said Mrs. Dagnitz. But you could tell that she'd figured out that all this hollering wasn't going anywhere.

"Just tell me," she said, "were you at Kevin's? Yes or no."

"He works all day. He's not even home," I said.

"Is this another lie? This is exactly why lying is so

bad, so . . . pernicious," said Mrs. Dagntiz. We'd turned into a neighborhood in northwest Portland with narrow streets. Mrs. Dagnitz leaned forward, looking for a place to park. I could tell she was losing the will to lecture me.

"What's 'pernicious'?" I asked.

"It's . . . it's . . . Could I fit into that space, do you think? I can't believe the parking around here. I've really gotten out of practice parallel parking . . ."

The truth is Mrs. Dagnitz had never been a good parallel parker. She would back up traffic for blocks, then get the car stuck half in, half out of some tiny space meant only for a motorcycle. She asked Mark Clark to do the parking. She leaped outside and stood on the curb and made a big show of directing him into the spot.

"Thanks," I said.

"Where were you?" he asked. He easily steered the car back into the spot with one hand.

"With this kid I know named Angus. He let me borrow his scooter to get home, because he didn't want me to get into more trouble than I was already in."

"Cool scooter," said Mark Clark.

I heaved a huge sigh, but before I got out of the car, Mark Clark put his hand on my arm. "Listen, I know she can be annoying, but she's right, or half right, actually. Lying sucks because—"

"I know, I know, the boy who cried wolf," I said.

"Exactly, but think about it for a minute," he said

quickly. Mrs. Dagnitz was standing on the curb, waiting. "Knowing you and what you've been up to lately, the day will come when you're going to need someone to believe you, and if you keep lying, no one will."

Dr. Lozano had moved offices since my last checkup. She used to be near the Rose Garden, where I saw Green Day play last fall, but now she was in a big brick medical building up the street from Twenty-third Avenue, a street of small, fancy shops that sell stuff you always want but never need: fancy soap, pointy high-heel shoes, bedsheets from France, and brightly painted plates from Italy.

Mrs. Dagnitz, Mark Clark, and I turned off Twenty-third and trudged uphill toward Dr. Lozano's office. I instantly started getting a sweaty head. If it had been Mark Clark driving, we'd have circled the building to see if there was parking closer to the air-conditioning of Dr. Lozano's office. But Mrs. Dagnitz grabbed the first place she saw. I really wished she'd go back to Santa Fe. People said having a dog was too much work, but it was much easier taking care of Ned than having a mother.

Mrs. Dagnitz hustled into the office ahead of us and said, "Minerva Clark is here to see Dr. Lozano." She made it sound as if I were the president.

Why does she do that? Why does she do anything? It was very air-conditioned. My legs got instant goose bumps. I should have changed into pants. Oh well. One good thing about having been so late—I escaped the world of shoes for another day. Mark Clark and I grabbed a *Highlights* magazine and started doing the Hidden Pictures puzzle. This is a doctor's-office tradition. We race to see who can find all the pencils, spoons, and scissors first. The loser has to buy the winner an ice cream. Even when I lose, Mark Clark buys the ice cream.

I'd found the canoe (in the branches of a tree) and Mark Clark had found the saw (in the side of a wooden cart) when Dr. Lozano called us back into her office. She wore skinny black pants, black low-tops, and a blue-and-black-striped blouse. She'd traded her gold nose ring for a ruby. She had to be the coolest doctor in the city. Dr. Lozano led the way, followed by Mrs. Dagnitz, who carried her giant purse over her arm as if she were the queen and complimented Dr. Lozano on the wall art. She acted as if she'd been here a million times before, when it had been Mark Clark who had brought me to see Dr. L. after my accident and every time since.

Dr. Lozano led us to her office instead of an exam room. The walls were painted dark coral, and pictures of wild mustangs were on the wall. There were two chairs across from her desk, and I plopped down in one. Mark Clark fetched another one from the other side of the room for Mrs. Dagnitz. I'd been trying to calm myself down after having been persecuted by

Mrs. Dagnitz ("persecuted"—one of last years spelling words—"to oppress or harass with ill-treatment"), and only now did I begin to feel excited.

Dr. Lozano had invited me to go with her to a big national meeting of brain doctors in New York City. I didn't know what it was, exactly, but we would fly together to New York and stay in a hotel with room service and a minibar.

"I thought it would be a good thing to sit down and discuss the conference and the trip, and what Minerva here can expect. As Mark may have told you, Mrs. Clark"—Awkward! Dr. Lozano obviously hadn't gotten the memo that Mother Dear was now Mrs. Dagnitz, married to Rolando of the man braid and yoga pants—"this is the annual meeting of the American Association of Neurologists. There'll be more than five thousand neurologists from all over the world. I'm going to be presenting a paper on the effect of trauma on the mind of the young adolescent, focusing on Minerva's accident and subsequent personality change."

"That sounds fascinating," said Mrs. Dagnitz. "What will Minerva have to do to prepare? Should she wear something nice?"

Dr. Lozano smiled and flipped open a file folder. "What will happen is that I will get up and tell the story of how I met Minerva, and her trauma from electric shock, and what I think has happened to her—from a neurological perspective—and then I'll ask Minerva to join me at the podium for a question-and-answer session. She should wear whatever she feels comfortable in."

"Well, what with her . . . personality change, that's just about anything!" Mrs. Dagnitz wailed. "I'm sick to death of seeing her in those high-top tennis shoes. They do nothing to flatter a big foot."

I took that opportunity to throw my feet up on the desk and show off my brand-new turquoise Chucks.

"Minerva, put your feet down this instant."

I put them down. I liked Dr. Lozano, and I was going to New York with her. I didn't want her to think I was an insufferable brat.

"There's something else," said Dr. Lozano. "This week I received a phone call from a producer at *Late Night with Seamus O'Connor*. He wants to do an interview with Minerva."

"Really?" I said.

"How cool is that?" asked Mark Clark. He reached across Mrs. Dagnitz's lap and punched my leg. "Min's going to be famous."

"An interview?" asked Mrs. Dagnitz doubtfully. She sat up straighter in her chair. "What kind of an interview? Isn't that the show where people with strange professions come on and O'Connor mocks them?"

"Actually, I don't watch it," said Dr. Lozano. "It's on much too late for me. But the producer is apparently married to a neurologist and heard about Minerva's transformation. He's curious to talk to a thirteen-year-old with true self-esteem."

"But this isn't true self-esteem. She was the victim of an unfortunate accident. She could have died!"

Why was Mrs. Dagnitz making such a production about this? I traded glances with Mark Clark behind her back. My look said, help me out a little here. Because Mark Clark had known me from birth, he could read it quite easily.

"I don't think Dr. Lozano would say yes to anything that wasn't good for her patient, Mom," said Mark Clark.

"It'll be fun," said Dr. Lozano. She picked up the phone and dialed a number listed in the folder. "And while I'm thinking of it, I've got to call the conference organizers to make sure they've got Minerva's name on the program. Another patient of mine had an accident similar to Minerva's, but at the last minute we decided Minerva was a better representative of— Oh yes, hello!"

We never heard what, exactly, I was a better representative of, because Dr. Lozano had at that moment gotten through to the conference person who was in charge of making the change on the program. She spelled my name out, M-I-N-E-R-V-A, to make sure the person on the other end of the line got it right.

Going to New York was the sort of thing that made me see how it wouldn't be so bad to be a grown-up. The problem was, in adulthood, there were many more lame and boring phone calls—like the one Dr. L. was making now—than there were fun trips to big cities that featured appearances on late-night television shows. What I really wanted to do in New York was go to the Metropolitian Museum of Art and see the mummies, and buy a cute fake purse. Chelsea de Guzman said you could buy a cute fake purse on the sidewalk for twenty dollars.

As we waited for Dr. Lozano to finish her call, I thought about how if you were a celebrity, you had other people to make the phone calls, and that's probably why every person I knew wanted to be famous. If you were famous, you could avoid the boring bits.

After Dr. Lozano hung up, we talked about airplane tickets and what the weather was going to be like, and whether I should get my hair straightened for the occasion (Mrs. Dagnitz), and what was actually going to be expected of me at the conference (Mark Clark), and then we were all standing up, and Dr. L. shook hands with my mother and brother, and hugged me, and said she was counting the days, and we were ushered back out of her air-conditioned office and into the insane-making heat.

- 5 -

We left Dr. Lozano's air-conditioned office and tromped back down the hill, crossing Twenty-fifth Avenue, where the car was parked, and on to Twenty-third Avenue. Mrs. Dagnitz bounced along, chattering about how this part of the city always reminded her of a college town, with its huge old three-story houses and wraparound porches. Most of the tiny front yards had been turned into flower gardens, overrun with yellow daisies and spiky purple flowers, and rosebushes that someone had paid a lot of attention to until several weeks ago, when the temperature pushed into the hundreds and people lost the drive to do anything but go in search of air-conditioning.

Mrs. Dagnitz and Mark Clark walked ahead of me in lockstep. Mark Clark always matched his step to the person he was walking with. One day I hoped to see him walk down the street with an old and proper Japanese lady wearing a kimono and high-heeled flip-flops—then what would he do? They swung down the hill, chattering about the best airline to fly to New York and about frequent-flier miles from some credit card. I knew if the discussion about airline tickets got too far down the road, they would forget all about getting ice cream.

"Mark Clark said we were going to get ice cream," I said.

"I could go for some mango gelato," said Mrs. Dagnitz.

We turned right on Twenty-third, nearly colliding with a lady and her two chocolate Labradors, panting in the heat.

"Don't their tongues look like bologna?" I said.

"Don't say that!" said Mrs. Dagnitz.

"Why not?"

"It's disgusting," said Mrs. Dagnitz. She looked at Mark Clark. "Tell me you're not keeping lunch meat in the house."

Mark Clark opened his mouth, then closed it without saying anything, which was fine with Mrs. Dagnitz, who stopped to look in a small shop that sold only cotton T-shirts and cotton pants in pale colors. A clothesline was strung across the inside of the narrow window with a single pale yellow T-shirt clipped to it with wooden clothespins. I felt like saying something snotty about how if she cared so much about Casa Clark being all poisoned by lunch meat, she could come home and monitor the fridge, but it was too hot to shoot my mouth off. My neck beneath my hair was drenched with sweat. I wished I'd put it in a braid.

Next to the cotton-only shop was the Vespa store. I peered in the window at a candy-apple-red scooter and thought about Angus Paine's Go-Ped lying in plain sight in the back of Mrs. Dagnitz's Pathfinder. I hoped no one had tried to steal it.

We continued on, past a fancy taqueria that smelled of fried tortillas and blared soft rock, and a shop that sold handmade soap that looked like pastries, and then a real pastry shop. If Mrs. Dagnitz hadn't stopped in front of the bath shop to marvel at a huge block of black soap, I wouldn't have noticed the sign in the window of the pastry shop: VISIT US SOON AT OUR NEW LOCATION AT 222 S.W. CORBETT.

I stared at that 222, three twos all in a row, like a stuck key on a keyboard. Why was it familiar? Corbett Street Grocery was on Southwest Corbett. Just as the thought began to form itself in my mind that Southwest Corbett was a neighborhood of small, brightly painted hippie houses, and that the grocery was the only store on that stretch of street, I saw the address letters bolted beside the cinder-black front door of the grocery, the iron address letters with their eerie rainbow sheen.

Could it be?

I looked up at the sign painted on the inside of the

window: Paisley's on 23rd. Was Paisley's on 23rd moving into the grocery, or what had been the grocery before the fire?

My palms felt itchy with possibility. I needed to go in there and do something—I didn't know what. I peered inside the window. At the far end two pastry cases formed an L. No one was at the register. A ceiling fan hung from the ceiling, twirling like a tired ballerina. I'd hoped they also sold ice cream, or frozen yogurt, or something so I could drag Mrs. Dagnitz and Mark Clark inside, but there was nothing but pastries, lined up in neat rows on trays behind the glass.

I glanced over at Mrs. Dagnitz. She was still transfixed by the chunk of black soap, as if it were a rock from another planet, which it looked as if it could have been. She sighed and said she wished they had this particular shop in Santa Fe. She wondered if she should go in right now and splurge on some of the black soap, or whether she should come back later. Mark Clark glanced down at his watch. He would stand there forever and let our mother blather on about the stupid soap. I had an idea.

"Come on," I said. "I need some shampoo and conditioner. Maybe there's something in here that can get rid of the frizzies." I threw open the door and went inside, passing through an invisible wall of pure odor—fruits, flowers, herbs, cinnamon, vanilla, the beach on a breezy day, and that smell hippie girls love that I can never pronounce. Working here would give your nose a heart attack. How did anyone do it? Mrs. Dagnitz came right in behind me, stepping accidentally on my heel. I may have become a stranger to Mrs. Dagnitz since she'd been gone, but in a few basic ways she was no stranger to me. She loved buying anything that you could carry away in a cute little handled bag.

Mark Clark planted himself just inside the door. The longer Mrs. Dagnitz was in town, the more he just went along with the program. He picked up a piece of plum-colored soap and put it down without smelling it. He stuck his hands in his pockets.

Mrs. Dagnitz grabbed a basket just inside the door and started filling it up with bath bombs and tubes of cream and hunks of that frightening black soap, happy as could be.

"Oh," I said, making a show of looking around with a frantic expression. I wrapped my arms across my stomach, hoping to make my situation look desperate, as if I might be on the verge of food poisoning. "I really need to use the bathroom." I scurried over to the clerk and asked whether they had a restroom. She looked up from where she was piling pink squares of bath salt in a tower. She said sorry—but there was a Starbucks three doors down. Thank you, surly counter-helper girl!

"Ohnnn," I said, scurrying back toward the front door, where Mrs. Dagnitz was smelling a tangerine-colored bath bomb twice the size of a real tangerine. I bent over like a bad actor doing a hunchback impersonation. "I'll be right back," I said.

Mrs. Dagnitz placed the bath bomb back in the bin and looked at me, her tanned face expressionless. I could tell she was trying to figure out what was going on with me. Finally she said, "Mark, go with her."

"I'm all right!" I said, pulling the door open and hurrying out before Mark Clark could say a word to anyone. I didn't know what I would do if he followed me, since I had no intention of going to Starbucks.

Before entering Paisley's on 23rd, I stopped to reread the sign in the window three times to make sure I wasn't seeing things, to double-check that the business was moving SOON to 222 S.W. Corbett, and not 1222 N.W. Corbett or 2222 S.E. Corbett.

VISIT US SOON AT OUR NEW LOCATION AT 222 S.W. CORBETT, the sign said in blue marker. I was positive that was the address of Angus Paine's family grocery. I stood there for a minute, wondering whether I should text Angus to double-check the address, or whether I would just be using that as an excuse to text him. Why would I want to text him anyway? I already had a boyfriend. Would Kevin care if I was sending random texts to another boy, even if it was a boy I was solving a mystery for? And was I actually solving a mystery for Angus Paine? Hadn't I just said a few hours earlier that I didn't think there was any mystery to be solved? I shook my head like a dog after a bath, to clear my mind of troubling thoughts that would only slow me down.

Inside, I hurried to the counter and stared down through the glass at a tray of pale yellow snickerdoodles, as if I might want to buy some. It was way too hot for cookies, too hot for anything. The tired ceiling fan stirred around the smells of vanilla and butter.

Where was the counter person, anyway? The longer I stood there, the more wiggly I got. I bounced first one leg, then the other. Any minute now my mother would be standing on the sidewalk, her hands on her hips, staring at me through the pastry shop's big window. I looked back over my shoulder, back out the window. Nothing. Two girls in baggy shorts straggled past, each carrying an icy coffee drink.

I drummed my fingers on the glass counter. Once Mrs. Dagnitz had purchased her soap, she'd be wondering where I'd gotten off to, and why I wasn't back, and what was going on here, had I really needed to use the bathroom or was I just using it as an excuse to run off and call my boyfriend. She sometimes talked about my brothers with their short attention spans, but they had inherited them from her. She was worse than a ferret—obsessed to death about one thing until a minute or two later she was obsessed about something else.

Finally a tall blond man in a white apron came out from the back, wiping his floury hands on his chest. His hair was the same color as the snickerdoodles, and he wore it in a small ponytail. His face was long and pale, his hands were long and pale, everything was long and pale, like an elf from one of Mark Clark's video games.

"So hey," I said, "when are you guys moving?"

"Moving?" he said. He scratched his head, then wrapped his arms around his skinny middle. I could tell he didn't know what I was talking about.

"I saw the sign. In the window."

"Oh, right!" He smiled. His front teeth overlapped. "Not sure. Was supposed to be next month, but now we're just not sure. Can I get you something?"

"Isn't that where the Corbett Street Grocery is? At 222 Southwest Corbett?"

"Where what is?"

"Where you're moving?" Adults could be so irritating. They always got on you about the tone of your voice, never stopping to think that if they weren't so annoying, you wouldn't be forced to give tone. Either Mr. Elf-Man was just the baker and really didn't know anything, or he was hiding what he knew, and why would he do that?

"You'd have to ask Paisley," he said. "She'll be in tomorrow."

I thanked the baker, then scooted out the door and into the heat. I could feel his curious stare on my back.

I'd beat cheeks out of there not a moment too soon. Mark Clark and Mrs. Dagnitz walked out of the soap store just as I walked out of the pastry shop.

Mrs. Dagnitz stopped. "Weren't you going to Starbucks?"

"I thought they'd have one in there," I said. "It was closer."

"The Starbucks restrooms are always so nice," said Mrs. Dagnitz. "They're so reliable. They always have a nice piece of art and plenty of toilet paper."

"This one was fine," I said. Why did I bother to say anything?

"You should stick to the Starbucks," she said. "It's a known entity, and known is always better than unknown."

I shut up. I fell into step behind Mark Clark. We continued our search for gelato, which I didn't even want anymore. Didn't Mrs. Dagnitz know anything about me? That for me, now, the unknown was better? Or at least more interesting? There are three gelato shops on Twenty-third, but only one of them was acceptable to Mrs. Dagnitz, for some reason I didn't listen to, something to do with one hundred percent organic something, or recycled whatnot. But the acceptable gelato shop didn't have any gelato that day because their refrigeration was broken. We drove home with all the windows rolled down. Mrs. Dagnitz had an attack of guilt over using the air-conditioning because it contributed to global warming. I was all for it. Doing our part to keep the polar ice caps good and frozen meant it was too loud to talk, which meant too loud for Mrs. Dagnitz to talk. Her wedding reception was on Saturday. Because I knew I would feel too guilty, I kept myself from counting the hours and days until she cut her second second-wedding cake and would go home to Santa Fe.

Kevin showed up on his bike just as I was finishing the dishes. We'd had leftover halibut (yuck!), which I'd snuck to Ned, praying to St. Francis of Assisi that there would be no bones. Did dogs choke on bones like people did?

Through the window over the sink I saw Kevin fly up the driveway on his little bike. Usually, just the sight of Kevin made my internal organs feel as if they were part of a dolphin show, flipping and spinning. But not when I saw him on his bike. He was the largest boy I knew, and he rode the smallest bike. Why? I wrung out the sponge and set it on the window ledge. Mrs. Dagnitz went insane when someone left a soggy sponge in the sink. Ned was sprawled on the kitchen floor by his water bowl, panting. I never realized corgis had such thick coats. I nudged him and he rolled over. I pet his tummy with my foot.

My middle older brother, Quills, appeared from upstairs, his bass guitar case dangling from one hand. The case was long and black, sinister looking, as if it held a deadly weapon inside and not a musical instrument. Quills poked me in the side to see if he could get me to jump, then looked out the window as Kevin leaned his bike against a tree. Together, we watched as Kevin answered his cell.

"Don't do anything I wouldn't do," he said. "But if you do, don't let Mom find out."

"Can you believe she changed her name to Dagnitz?" I said. "Deedee Dagnitz."

"Yeah, well," he said.

"She's driving me totally insane," I said. "Was she always this perky-weird, or is it all the yoga?"

"The yoga's actually made her better," said Quills. He'd put his case down and tore a spotty banana from the bunch on top of the fridge. "Where is she, anyway?"

"They went to a movie, then back to their hotel. But she will see me bright and early in the morning, so she can get in a full day of making me want to pluck out my own eyes." I picked up the sponge from the window ledge and squeezed it again with all my might. If it had been a live sponge, I would have killed it.

Quills left for band practice without saying when he would be back. Normally, he would have said when he was coming home—he would have left the time on a scrap of paper and stuck it under one of the plastic bug magnets on the fridge. Now that Mrs. Dagnitz was back, he acted as if he could do as he pleased, as if we didn't need to know where he was going and when he would be back.

From the computer room across the hall I could hear cartoon swords clashing, Mark Clark on his video game killing his pretend monsters.

I snagged two Otter Pops from the big box in the

freezer and pretend ice-skated into the backyard, where Kevin sat on the picnic bench picking at a scab on his knee. It was twilight, the Purpley Time, as I used to call it when I was little. I brought him a red Otter Pop, rested it on his bare thigh. Red was his favorite flavor. Red was everyone's favorite flavor. I hated to say this about Kevin, but he pretty much liked everything every other boy I knew liked. World of Warcraft. X-Men movies. McDonald's Big Macs. Skechers. He'd told me he was taking Japanese next year, which I thought made him a brainiac nerd like Reggie, but it turned out that it was just because the teacher was supereasy. Was this bad? Considering he had the most killer deep-mountain-lake-blue eyes?

Kevin tore the top of his Otter Pop open with his teeth. We started a debate about which Otter Pops were better, the red ones or the green ones. Otter Pops are just colored frozen sugar water in a plastic tube, but we compared flavors like we were world-famous creators of frozen confections.

"Green is far superior because it mingles the flavor of sugar, water, and green dye," I said.

"Red is the Otter Pop flavor of Nickelback," said Kevin. "It's pure bombdiggity goodness."

"Green is a cool color, and makes you feel cooler when you eat it."

"Red is better because it just tastes better," he said.

"That's just your opinion," I said. "You need

evidence to back it up." I sounded like my dad, Charlie, the lawyer.

Kevin sucked on his Otter Pop and shrugged. I got the feeling it was too much trouble for him to think up an answer. He had come over straight after his manny job. Smears of chocolate stained the thighs of his khaki shorts, and Harvey or Otis had drawn a two-headed snake on the back of his hand.

Even though Kevin had been my boyfriend for a while now, it still was strange having him show up at my house. When Kevin showed up, I had to stop whatever I was doing and have a conversation, and there was always the big question of whether we'd kiss. Chelsea de Guzman always had boyfriends, but mostly they just texted back and forth hundreds of times a day. They talked on the phone. They IMed. It was as if her boyfriends lived in Mozambique and this was the only way they could communicate. I knew for a fact that one of her boyfriends lived three blocks away. Still, this arrangement seemed a lot less stressful than having the boy turn up and sit on your picnic table and eat all your red Otter Pops.

Kevin was in the middle of a story about the twins and a praying mantis they had found on a shrub when who should blast up the driveway on his skateboard but my best friend, Reggie. He wore a backwards baseball cap and a baggy T-shirt that said, CALL ME GEEK TODAY, BOSS TOMORROW.

"S'up?" said Reg.

"Hey," I said.

"Hey," said Kevin.

Then, silence. Kevin concentrated on slurping the last bit of melted red juice from the bottom of his Otter Pop, and Reg concentrated on flipping the end of his skateboard with his toe.

Can I just say—awkward!

The first time Kevin ever flew up our driveway on his little bike, Reg and I were sitting on the kitchen floor messing around with Ned, tying a red bandanna first around his neck, turning him into a gunslinger (Rootin' Tootin' One-Eyed Ned), and then around his chin, turning him into an old lady (Gramma Neddy). Reg was the king of impersonations. He has a great old-granny voice. Kevin has a great big high horse he sits on once in a while. Is it because he is tall, and a swimmer? He leaned against the sink and texted a friend, refusing to join in the fun. Later that very night, Kevin IMed me that Reg was a dweeb and Reg IMed me that Kevin was a tool.

I couldn't think of anything to do but tell Reg what was s'up. He asked, didn't he? Kevin knew about Angus Paine, but Reggie didn't. I told him how Angus had seen the article about me in the paper, and called to see if I could help him solve the mystery of who had burned down his family's haunted grocery, which was already a mysterious place because it had its own ghost, who lived in the walk-in freezer. I told how Robotective with the voice from *2001* and the glass eye thought it was an accident, and how Angus was positive it *wasn't*, and how the whole thing was getting weirder by the minute because just as I was thinking I agreed with Robotective, I ran across Paisley's on 23rd, which had a sign in the window saying the business was taking over the same space as the grocery, when that was totally impossible.

"But it's not impossible," said Reg. He'd set his skateboard against the side of the house, had found the basketball in the woodpile by the garage, and had started shooting baskets. "Businesses move around all the time. There's that gas station on Sandy across from the Jack in the Box that's now a bank."

"But if Paisley's was moving there, that would mean that Angus's family was selling the store, and the way he made it sound, they were totally never selling it. The reason it's so important that it be ruled arson and not an accident is so they can get the insurance money to fix it and then reopen it. That grocery store is, like, their whole lives."

"You still get insurance money if it's an accident," said Kevin. He watched Reg make a jump shot. Reg was a brain, not a jock, but his house also had its own hoop bolted over the garage, and shooting baskets was something he did when he was stuck on a computer coding problem.

"Not nearly as much," I said.

"Who discovered the fire? 'Cause you know what

they say about arson. The one who smelt it dealt it," said Kevin.

Reg snorted, dribbled toward the basket, and performed a perfect jump shot, nothing but net. I kept waiting for Kevin to lope on over and steal the ball, but he just sat there, folding and unfolding the Otter Pop's empty plastic sleeve. "No lie, dude," said Kevin. "With arson, the one who reports it is usually the one who set it."

"Are you a junior fireman or something?" said Reg. "Where's your dalmatian?"

"Are you always such a freakin' tool?" asked Kevin. "Min obviously needs our help here."

Reg spun around and shot me the ball, which I caught without flinching. If you have three older brothers and a basketball hoop, you learn how to do this while you are still in diapers.

"Minerva doesn't need our help, dude. She *owns* us when it comes to this stuff. But then, you wouldn't know that, would you?" Reg glared at Kevin from under his wavy bangs.

What was he on about? I tuned out while they tossed low-grade insults at each other. Kevin said he didn't know how I could stand Reg, who was a know-it-all jerk, and Reg said at least he knew something, which was more than he could say about Kevin.

It was almost dark. The security light came on over the garage. Reg challenged Kevin to a game of horse. I could have joined in, but I needed to sort some things out. I took over Kevin's spot on the picnic table and stared out at the tree-enshrouded yard.

I wrapped my elbows around my shins, rested my chin on my knees, and thought about Paisley's on 23rd, how sleepy it had been in there, as if they hadn't had a customer all day. I remember looking down into the glass case and noticing the neat rows of snickerdoodles. Freshly baked that morning and not one had been purchased. It had been head-sweaty hot, there was no doubt about it, but on our way home we'd driven past a shop that sold nothing but fancy cupcakes and it was packed. People had even been sitting outside on the spindly little metal chairs, licking off the frosting and sighing with delight. If it was too hot for cookies, it was too hot for cupcakes, right?

All I know about business is what I learned from having a lemonade stand with Reggie one summer when we were in fourth grade. We'd persuaded our moms to let us sell fresh squeezed. That would be our selling point. We wrote FRESH-SQUEEZED! in the corners of our sign in lemony-yellow letters outlined in red. When we hardly sold any, we got the idea that maybe we needed a new street corner. We moved the operation from Reggie's corner to my corner, and business picked up a little. That was probably what Paisley was thinking, that if she moved to another corner, she'd sell more snickerdoodles. Maybe that's why she was moving her business to 222 S.W. Corbett. I'd go back in the morning and talk to her. In the meantime, I wanted to call Angus Paine and grill him about what was going on. Were his parents selling the building or what? And why hadn't he told me? Wasn't that sort of *major*?

I was thinking so hard I hadn't noticed it had gotten dark. The trees in our yard must have been a hundred feet tall. They'd been there before there were houses around here, and most of these houses were a hundred years old. They blocked out the streetlight. They blocked out all light. Just as I was thinking it was downright horror-movie creepy under our backyard canopy of leafy branches, I flashed on the image of Angus's Grams, or whoever she was, burned to a crisp, glued to her chair by her polyester pants, and just as I was trying to shake that horrible image from my head, something hit my arm.

"Ow!" What the . . . !

I had to crane my neck around to find Reg and Kevin, over on the far side of the basket, about as far away from me as they could possibly be and still be able to make a shot. Something else hit me in the middle of my chest. The sharp, pyramid-shaped rock fell into my lap. I peered into the dark yard. Behind the trees ran a low white picket fence. There was a narrow break between two trees on the sidewalk side of the backyard, and I could just make out what looked like someone on a bike.

"Hey!" I yelled out. "When I tell my three older

brothers that someone's throwing rocks at me, it's really going to suck to be you!"

With that the kids—it turned out to be three of them—tore past on their bikes.

"You suck, Minerva Clark, you big snitch!" Then they fell all over themselves giggling, and one of their bikes crashed over, and one of the kids swore at one of the other ones. Then suddenly Reg sped past me, running down the driveway shouting and waving his hands like some lunatic cowboy trying to get his cows to move. "Mwahahahahaha!" shouted Reg, chasing the kids down the street.

"What was up with *that?*" said Kevin.

"I'd say it was the fifth graders who TPed my friend Chelsea's house a while back."

"Why'd they call you a snitch?"

"They got the TP from the storage closet at school. I told Mrs. Grumble. She's the recess monitor for the lower grades. She was in the army before she came to our school."

"So you *are* a snitch," said Kevin. I could tell he thought that was tragically uncool.

"Yeah, I am. There is never any toilet paper in the middle school girls' bathroom, and I'm totally sick of it."

We strolled down to the end of the drive. The streetlight showed two dripping patches of yellow on the side of my house. The fifth graders had tossed a few eggs before Reg chased them off.

"Looks like you made some enemies," said Kevin.

"You can hardly call fifth graders enemies," I said. "More like an infestation."

I was grateful to hear Kevin laugh. A lot of times I cracked what I thought was a pretty good joke and he just stood there looking at me.

- 6 -

It was the dead middle of the night and the temperature in my room was at least a hundred. I was getting to an age where I understood the grown-up complaint—if it just weren't so *humid*. It was global warming right there on the third floor of Casa Clark, Portland, Oregon, USA, Earth, Milky Way, Universe. The windows in my third-floor room were thrown open as wide as they could possibly go, but there was not the smallest sigh of breeze. I lay on my hot mattress in my pink SHE WANTS REVENGE T-shirt, my hair stuck on top of my head with a scrunchie, an orange Otter Pop bent around my throat. It was meant to cool the blood in the vein that ran up the side of my neck and into my head, tricking me into imagining I actually was cool, when in reality it was so hot I could probably hard-boil an egg beneath my armpit.

Before I had laid myself down to slow-roast in my stuffy room, I had moved Jupiter's cage down to the basement, where it was at least twenty degrees cooler. Ferrets can't take this kind of heat. I felt lonely, even though Jupiter usually kept me awake half the night playing with his red-and-green plastic ball. Or enjoying a midnight snack, which meant pushing his food bowl around with his nose until he ran into the side of the cage and tipped it over, sending pellets of the kitten food he loved cascading down through the wire bars. When the pellets hit the wood floor, they bounced around like the beads of a broken necklace. Then Ned appeared and Hoovered up all the kitty chow, which gave him the worst gas.

I flung myself around, then threw my arms over my head. Maybe if I got them as far away from me as possible, I'd stop sweating. This was lame. The Otter Pop bent around my neck was not making me cooler, just crabbier. I flung the thing across my room, got up, and went downstairs, thinking I'd crash on the living room sofa, but the second my bare legs came into contact with the scratchy upholstery, I realized I could never fall asleep there. Why did I have to be so hot? Why did Mrs. Dagnitz have to be so annoying? Why hadn't Angus Paine told me his parents had sold their store to Paisley of Paisley's on 23rd? I was figuring this out about people who wanted mysteries solved—they never told you the whole truth. I wandered into the kitchen and got a Mountain Dew, then went to the computer room, where I fired up Mark Clark's PC and Googled "Paisley's on 23rd."

There weren't many listings. She had a Web site under construction. One review on CitySearch.com said that the napoleons at Paisleys on 23rd were the best in Portland. There was an article in the paper about Paisley O'Toole catering a party for an organization that helped find jobs for people who'd been in car wrecks, and another one about the special green oatmeal cookies she baked in honor of St. Patrick's Day. There was nothing about the bakery's move to 222 S.W. Corbett, or really, anything of any interest at all.

On impulse, I texted Angus Paine: U didn't say ur rents were selling the store.

Just as I was drinking the last of my Mountain Dew, my phone rang. *Oooo-oooo-oooo-ahhnn!* Thumpa-thumpa-thumpa. *Oooo-oooo-oooo-ahhnn!* Thumpa-thumpa-thumpa. I choked on the soda, practically spitting up on the keyboard. Who was calling me at one thirty in the morning?

Angus Paine, of course.

"What are you doing?" I asked, still coughing and gasping for breath.

"Got your text," he said, as if it were one thirty in the afternoon. He lowered his voice, all flirt monster–like. "I was thinking about you."

"You were?"

"About our mystery," he said. "I really wish I could get you to see it was arson. What would I have to do to make that happen?"

"Giving me all the facts would be good, just for starters. Why didn't you tell me your parents sold the building to the lady who owns Paisley's on 23rd?"

Angus was silent for a few seconds, so silent I thought I'd lost him.

"Hello?" I was irritated.

"Wait, I'm trying to understand this here."

"Paisley O'Toole," I said, "who's moving her pastry shop from Northwest Twenty-third to 222 Southwest Corbett."

"That's our address," said Angus.

"I *know*. That's my *point*." Was he playing dumb? I thought only girls played dumb.

"You're not talking about the lady who's opening the Artery Hardening Department?"

"Artery Hardening Department?" Suddenly I felt tired. My stomach gurgled and sighed like a haunted house. It was a result of Mountain Dew on an empty stomach in the middle of the night. It was the result of Angus Paine acting like a complete and utter tool.

He laughed. "It's what my parents call the dessert section that's going in by the deli. You know how now grocery stores have, like, a little shrunken Starbucks right inside the front door? That's the concept. Nat and

Nat thought it would help business to have some really smokin' sweet stuff, gourmet like. Right now they only stock those vegan cookies that taste like dog biscuits. They thought they needed to offer something that was actually edible."

I wanted to laugh, but I wasn't going to give Angus Paine the satisfaction. "So Paisley O'Toole who owns Paisley's on 23rd has not bought the grocery from your parents?"

"You're one tough chick, Minerva."

"Excuse me, but could you be more random?"

"That was one of my best jokes, about the cookies tasting like dog biscuits. Most girls crack up. But you're not most girls, are you?"

What was I supposed to say to this? I muttered something about the sign in the window at Paisley's shop.

Angus Paine laughed with what I thought was too much relief, but I couldn't be sure. "Dude, I thought I told you, this grocery has been in our family for—"

"Yeah, I know, forever."

"—for generations. I'm going to take it over as soon as I graduate from college. My dad wants me to go to a four-year college. I could try to go the community college route, but . . ."

Blah blah blah blah blah. I stopped listening, which a sleuth should never do, I know, but it was so late.

"Did Paisley have a contract with your parents?" I interrupted him.

"You mean, did she have motivation to torch the place?"

Yes, that was exactly what I'd meant. People committed crimes for love or money. It was a well-known fact, at least on *Law & Order*. "Maybe she was so desperate to expand her business, she got into a situation where she was going to have to pay your parents more than she had."

"I never would have figured that out," said Angus. "It could be her. I bet it was. That makes total sense."

"But there's no hard evidence."

"I'll call Robotective tomorrow, let him find the evidence. That's his job, not our job, right?"

"If you want to get technical, none of this is our job," I said.

He laughed. "And hey, when am I going to get my wheels back?"

I remembered his Go-Ped, now stowed in our garage. A bad thing happened next. I felt excited. I felt glad to have an excuse to lay eyes on Angus Paine, he of the red hair, outrageous freckles, chipped front tooth, and geeky black trench coat. How could this be when I didn't even like him, and I already had a boyfriend?

In the morning I learned a secret about my brother Morgan. Even though he is a Buddhist who never raises his voice and has genuine conversations with Weird Rolando about composting, hybrid cars, and something called string theory, he was using my dog Ned as a babe magnet.

The day after I brought Ned home, Morgan started taking him for a walk every morning. Morgan had never been a big pet person, even though he was a vegetarian. You'd think that if he loved animals enough to give up hamburgers and chicken wings, he'd have taken more interest in the parade of animals who'd been through our house: Jupiter, of course, and all the rats, cats, rabbits, guinea pigs, fighting beta fish, and George and Gracie, our two ginormous brown poodles Mrs. Dagnitz took with her when she left, but he said one thing had nothing to do with the other. Morgan was a philosophy major in college and made mysterious statements like this all the time.

Then he fell in love with Ned and his foxy face and big ginger-colored splotches. He said that the way Ned smiled, he looked as if he was always about to burst into a show tune.

Morgan never asked anyone else to come along on his walks with Ned. I thought it was because he was a philosopher and needed his alone time to ponder ideas large and small.

Ha! Little did any of us know.

Earlier that morning when Morgan left Casa Clark with Ned, he ran smack into Mark Clark and me, standing on the sidewalk in front, gazing up at the toilet-paper streamers hanging from the trees, the shrubs, the fence, and the phone lines. We'd been TPed but good.

"Any idea who did this?" asked Mark Clark.

I pulled a strand of paper from where it was wrapped about the phone pole on the parking strip. Not two-ply. One-ply, and so scratchy you could give yourself a nasty rash if you weren't careful. It was toilet paper from my school.

"Fifth graders!" I said. "They have a vendetta against me."

"There's nothing worse than a fifth grader with a vendetta," said Mark Clark. He reach over and tugged my ponytail. I knew when I was being mocked.

"I'm not kidding." I told him how the paper was stolen from the supply closet at school, and how I'd already turned them in once for the same offense, and how the ringleader, Daniel Vecchio, was on some kind of medication for being pure evil. Whatever is beyond attention deficit disorder is what he had. He ate with his mouth so far open the food fell right out and back onto his plate. Fifth graders are almost beneath hating, but I hated Daniel Vecchio and he hated me.

Mark Clark laughed. Then, suddenly, there was Morgan and Ned. Despite his heavy coat and the brain-boiling heat, my dog looked as if he could walk a hundred miles on his stumpy white legs. The saying should be changed from "happy as a clam" to "happy as a dog on a walk."

Morgan set off in the opposite direction as if he hadn't seen us.

"Hey! Wait up!" I said.

I don't know why I wanted to join him. Morgan was usually gone for about an hour—fifty-nine minutes too long of a walk for me. But I was irritated at Mark Clark. I did not like being patronized. Now that he was a grown-up, he'd totally forgotten how rotten fifth-grade boys could be. Also, if I hung around too long, Mark Clark would make me clean up the toilet-paper mess.

Morgan and I tramped down the sidewalk. It was so hot he'd been forced to remove his trademark earflap hat. He'd talked about shaving his head, or else growing his hair to his waist like Weird Rolando. (I told him I would have to kill him first.) Morgan agonized over his hair, which was thin like Mrs. Dagnitz's. He was the only one of us who did not have enough hair for ten people. We walked along, stopping at every yard so Ned could sniff and lift.

"Why do dogs' tongues always look like bologna?" I asked.

"Don't know," he said.

"Do you think it's, like, evolutionary?"

"Could be," he said.

"I made that observation before and Mrs. Dagnitz lost it. To her, saying 'lunch meat' is the same as eating it."

"You should give her a break," said Morgan. "I know you're angry at her, but it's not easy being her age."

"Hey, I'm thirteen, officially the worst age in human existence. She gets no sympathy from me."

"Well, she should."

"Where are we *going*, anyway?" I asked. I knew a stroll when I was on one, and this was not a stroll. It was a march. We were clicking down the sidewalk like we'd just shoplifted something and were trying to flee the scene without drawing attention to ourselves. We were headed toward Fremont, a long street of small shops, coffee places that were Not Starbucks, a place that sold a thing called a wall bed, plus a place that served the best hamburgers in the city.

Also on Fremont was a pet store that sold the special all-natural kitty food we gave to Jupiter. "Can we stop by Green's for some Jupiter food? He's almost out."

"That pet shop?"

"Just past Roasted," I said. Roasted was one of the Not Starbucks coffee places. As soon as the word left my lips, Morgan perked up, as if I were a mystical healer from Java who had uttered the secret magic word of happiness. We turned onto Fremont a half block before Roasted, just in time to see a waitress clearing plates from one of the tiny tables on the sidewalk. She was short, with swingy blond hair and big arm muscles. She wore baggy khakis cut off just below the knee and a tank top that showed off her biceps.

"He-e-e-y," she called out as we approached, "it's

my favorite boys. You getting the regular today? Let me clear this stuff."

Morgan turned dark pink and ducked his head. "Hey, Jeannette. Not today. We're just . . ."

". . . on a real walk?" she called out, laughing. "Neddie thanks you, I'm sure. Hey, Neddie Teddy Bear! I LOVE that dog!" And then she hustled back into the coffee shop with her stack of dirty plates. At the sound of her voice, Ned wagged his stump. Ned *knew* her.

So Morgan hadn't been walking Ned at all. Morgan had been coming up to Roasted to have his "regular" served by Jeannette, who loved my dog, Neddie Teddy Bear.

I could have razzed Morgan until he lost his Buddha cool, but I was more interested in thinking about his secret. It wasn't a big secret—so he had a crush on a waitress with nice arm muscles—but it was a secret, one that Morgan, who was the brother who believed in honesty and karma, had easily kept from all of us.

All the way to Green's I thought about secrets. I thought about how until my accident, which had led me to solving mysteries, I'd thought I was the only one with secrets—that everyone else in my life said what they meant, and went where they said they were going, and did what they said they were going to do. We walked on in silence. Morgan's face returned to its normal pinky-beige color.

At Green's we bought a ten-pound bag of all-natural

kitty food. As Morgan paid Mrs. Green, who was about four hundred years old and had an English accent and called us both "Lovey," I mentioned that the food was for my ferret and she tried to sell us ferret chow, which was twice the price. I told her one of *my* secrets: that for half the price you can get cat food, and ferrets like it just as well.

Just as we left the shop, Morgan's cell rang. It was Mrs. Dagnitz, hollering about something. Mrs. Dagnitz always shouted into her cell phone, as if she couldn't trust the tiny receiver to project her voice. I could hear her from where I was giving Ned some water by the bike rack. Green's always kept a purple ceramic bowl full of water just outside.

Morgan clutched at his thin bangs and grimaced at me. "Oh right! Oh! Right! Yes. No. I'm sorry. No. Yes. We're so sorry! Could we tomorrow? Okay. Right. Right. Sorry. So sorry. Yes. No. No. Hello? Mom?"

Mrs. Dagnitz had hung up on him. On Morgan, the nicest brother, who was always telling us how we should cut her some slack. "We told her we'd go to yoga this morning."

"Oh," I said. Ned finished lapping up all the water in the bowl and grinned at me. I let him pull me back down the street, pretending he was going to pull my arm out of the socket.

"That private family yoga session. Some friend of hers set it up," said Morgan. He was the only one of us who'd ever done yoga besides Mrs. Dagnitz and Weird Rolando. I could just imagine Quills in some goofy upside-down pose, with all his change and guitar picks tumbling out of his pocket, and Mark Clark trying to touch his toes.

"Oh yeah," I said.

"They waited," said Morgan, "but left without us."

"Oh . . . that's . . ." The words "too bad" floated through my head, but I could not possibly say them. I started giggling. *Oh, I'm sorry to hear that*. Ha ha ha! *Oh no. And I really wanted to go to family yoga!* I wanted to be nice. I wanted to show Morgan that I was as kind and gentle as he was, but I couldn't do it.

I dropped Ned's leash I was laughing so hard. He jumped around, as if we were playing. I held my stomach. Ha ha ha hoo! A lady watering her lawn looked up and said, "Wish I could get in on the fun." Morgan scratched his head and started laughing, too. He didn't even know why, which made me laugh even harder. I bent over to pick up Ned's leash.

Mrs. Dagnitz and Weird Rolando and my brothers would be gone for hours. After yoga, they'd stop for muffins and smoothies somewhere, and Mrs. Dagnitz would need to stop by a store and buy something. Yoga always put her in a shopping frame of mind.

Now that there was no reason to hurry home, that's all I wanted to do. I made a plan in my head. Feed Jupiter and let him play with a plastic bag, then clean up some of the fifth graders' TP job, just to show I'd made the effort, then find Angus Paine and return his Go-Ped.

As we walked, I asked Morgan what he knew about arson and arsonists, and he said the mind of the arsonist is the most mysterious criminal mind there is, because arsonists are almost never caught, so few people ever get to study their personalities. If they're not setting a fire for insurance purposes, then usually they're setting it because they're angry.

"The strangest thing is that almost all arsonists are of below-average intelligence, except for a very small percentage who are of way-above-average intelligence. But most of the time, they're just angry kids."

"Kids?" I asked.

"Guys in their twenties," he said.

"Or maybe ladies in their forties who like to do yoga?"

Morgan put the kitty-food bag down in the middle of the sidewalk. The bag was pale green and had a huge white cat on it. He rubbed his shoulder. He was my most serious brother. I didn't think he'd get my joke, but he smiled and shook his head.

"She's not that bad," he said.

"She is too," I said, just to be a brat.

"Yeah, I know," said Morgan.

I played with Jupiter for the length of six songs on my laptop, then took a shower, washed my hair, put on my jean skirt and pink camouflage Chuck Taylors, and called Angus Paine. We agreed to meet at the grocery at noon.

This gave me plenty of time to whip on over to Paisley's on 23rd to talk to Paisley. I wanted to ask her about moving her shop, and what she was going to do now that there was nowhere to go. Was she upset? Relieved? I was sure I could tell by the look on her face whether she'd had anything to do with the fire.

Northwest Twenty-third wasn't far, but anytime you had to cross a bridge in Portland, it seemed far. To get to Northwest from Northeast meant crossing the rust-colored Broadway Bridge—through the grating you could see the green-gray waters of the Willamette far below—and passing through the Pearl District, with its art galleries, fancy furniture stores, beauty salons, and yoga studios. Our dad, Charlie, talks a lot about selling Casa Clark and buying a loft in the Pearl so he doesn't have to mow the lawn anymore, except he doesn't mow the lawn—Quills does. I had a moment of one hundred percent pure freak-out when I zipped past a long plate-glass window, glanced inside, and saw a small army of skinny people, the soles of their feet propped against the inside of their knees, palms pressed together prayer-style in the center of their heaving chests. Yoga! Was this where Mrs. Dagnitz liked to go? Was my family in there? I sped past without looking back.

By the time I reached Northwest Twenty-third, my hair was dry. I stuck it up on top of my head with a black chopstick I'd found in the silverware drawer. Inside Paisley's, a short lady with dark wavy hair and huge green eyes that looked at you like you were up to something was cleaning the top of the glass case with Windex. She had a tattoo on the inside of her wrist of a butterfly escaping from its cocoon. Quills was the family interpreter of meaningful tattoos, but I would say hers meant that she hoped to be reborn in a new job. "Excuse me, are you Paisley?"

"She has another doctor's appointment." The lady squirted the glass, then sighed.

"Oh. Okay."

She squinted up at me. "Can I get you something?"

I stared down through the glass at a row of oatmeal cookies. For some reason I thought of shingles on a roof. Not just a doctor's appointment, but *another* doctor's appointment? What do people go to the doctor for? I went to the doctor when I had ear infections. I went to the emergency room when I sprained my ankle during a Super Soaker fight in our driveway. But Paisley went to the doctor a lot. It was that word "another"—made it sound as if Paisley was always running off to the doctor, leaving the cranky butterfly-tattoo lady to mind the shop. Maybe Paisley had one of those grown-up diseases we learned about in health, like cancer or hardening of the arteries.

Or maybe she was seeing a psychiatrist-type doctor because she had done something bad. Like set a fire.

"Hello?" said Butterfly Tattoo in a POed tone of voice. "You want something or not?"

I knew I'd spaced out. "No . . . but thanks," I said. Just as I turned to go, she hurried around the counter and opened the door. "Here she is," she said.

Into the shop came a woman in an electric wheelchair. She wore white pants and a sheer lavender-and-pink paisley blouse. She looked only a little older than Mark Clark, who was turning twenty-six in a few days. One curled hand lay in her lap, and the other one operated the joystick on her chair.

Paisley of Paisley's on 23rd?

She and Butterfly Tattoo talked about business, about a late delivery of flour, and something about one of the mixers. Paisley of Paisley's on 23rd smelled like lavender. Butterfly Tattoo wanted next Thursday off. I stood there like the goofball I was. I should have been paying attention—a sleuth messes up when she fails to pay attention—but I couldn't keep from glimpsing at Paisley's curled hands. They were narrow and pale and useless-looking.

"Yes?" she was saying to me. She had white, even teeth, the kind I hoped to have after my braces came off.

"Oh," I said. "Oh."

"We're not hiring at the moment, but Michelle here

can give you an application if you'd like to fill one out. We keep them on file."

"I was wondering about your new location," I said. "About when you were moving."

"Not for a while now," she said.

"There was that fire," I said.

She didn't looked surprised that I knew, or as if I'd found her out. She didn't cut her eyes over to the side, or look down in her lap, or change the subject, or get all huffy and ask how I knew about the fire. She looked straight up into my face and said, "Yes, the fire. That kind of calamity is always so sad. Even though it wasn't Nat and Nat's home, still, they've put their heart and soul into that grocery. It's practically a Portland landmark." Paisley had huge gray eyes, like a Portland sky in early spring.

"Were you closing up this shop then?"

"Never!" sputtered Butterfly Tattoo, and then she laughed.

Paisley gave her the same patronizing look our science teacher Mr. Hale gives Reggie when he belches in class.

Paisley said, "I was hoping to open a small kiosk, where I'd have a limited menu, just some cookies and a few pastries. Now, of course, everything is on hold. But we're hoping to open in the fall."

"That must have cost you a lot of money," I said. I didn't know what I meant by *that*. It was one of the benefits of being thirteen. You could say something completely random and no one thought anything of it. I'd just tossed this out there to see if perhaps Paisley would get excited and say, "Oh yes! It was going to be so expensive . . ." Something to show that she was relieved that she wasn't going to have to spend the money to open the *kiosk*, whatever that was.

"I imagine normally it would have been, but Natalie was giving me the space for free. One of the benefits of growing up together. Actually, I was friends with Maureen, her youngest sister. Natalie was the oldest. They had one of those huge Catholic families."

Paisley talked on about the old neighborhood, and about the kinds of trouble she and Maureen used to get into. She talked about Maureen's kids, and about how she was the first person outside the family to hold Angus when he was born. She wouldn't let me leave without giving me a cookie and some raspberry seltzer water to take with me. She wanted to give me a half dozen cookies, but Butterfly Tattoo stepped in and said no.

I hopped back on Angus's Go-Ped and sped through downtown to Corbett Street Grocery. I carried my cookie and seltzer water in a small white paper bag, folded over at the top. Although it seemed like Paisley wasn't much of a businesswoman, giving away the profits to undercover do-it-yourself girl detectives, I knew she hadn't set the fire at the grocery. This gave me a bad case of swirled-around feelings. Paisley was cool, and so it was good she wasn't an arsonist. But if it wasn't Paisley who set the fire, who was it? And what would Angus say when I told him? I was relieved to find out he'd been telling the truth about Paisley's renting a small space at the grocery instead of taking it over completely. This didn't seem like a big deal, but it proved he wasn't a hedger, a person who was always trying to find a way not to tell the truth, without having to tell an outright lie.

I was about twenty minutes late and Angus still wasn't there. I leaned the Go-Ped against someone's garden wall and sat on the curb across from the grocery. I waited. I ate the snickerdoodle and drank the raspberry seltzer. There was a huge pink rose shrub on the parking strip filled with bumblebees, and they cruised me until I couldn't stand it. It was the cookie or my kiwi-scented hair conditioner. I wiped my hands on my legs, and just as I was about to walk across the street to the grocery, Robotective Huntington cruised by in a dark blue Dadmobile. He slowed the car, turned to look hard at me through his mirrored shades, then drove on.

I crossed behind the street, and as I got closer to the charred front door, I noticed that the door was ajar. I pushed it open with one finger. "Angus?" I called out into the gloom. Everything looked just as it had before—the piles of burned junk, the flap of soggy ceiling.

The whole place still smelled burned. It hurt your nose

to smell it. I wondered if it would always smell that way in the heat, even after Angus's parents, Nat and Nat, had the grocery rebuilt, or however you fixed a half-burned building. Debris crunched underfoot as I walked toward the back of the store, past the tall shelf with the row of shiny antique toasters. I stopped and stared up at them. One looked like a little drawer set on end, with the handle on top. Another one was sleek and square and looked like one of the messenger droids from *Star Wars*. I counted ten of them—who knew toast had such a history?

Then I heard footsteps overhead. I hadn't forgotten there was an apartment upstairs, but I'd let it drift to the back of my mind. It was easier to think about how, whether the fire was ruled an arson or an accident, Angus's family would be able to rebuild, and how all that was lost was a lot of snack food, meats and cheeses in the deli case, and newspapers piled in the wire stand beside the door. The footsteps upstairs made me think of the lady Angus said everyone called Grams, and how she had burned to death up there. They made me realize that if this was an arson and not an accident, the arsonist was also a murderer.

"Angus?" I called out, louder than necessary. It was Angus upstairs walking around, right? Not the murderer/arsonist, or even creepy Robotective Huntington, with the flat voice and strange off-kilter eyes. For a split second, I remembered the ghost. What did Angus call her? Louise. But she lived in the freezer, didn't she?

"Uh, NO, Minerva," I said aloud to the empty store. I believed in ghosts, but only as a joke. The same way I still said I believed in the tooth fairy, just for laughs. Or this was my official position.

At the rear of the store, across from the walk-in freezer I glimpsed the bottom steps of a narrow wooden staircase. The steps were painted red. It didn't look as if the fire had reached them. Before I could give it a thought, I marched over and took them two at a time, to the second floor.

The door at the top of the stairs had been burned off its hinges. The fire had done more damage up here than downstairs in the grocery. Everything was black or ashy gray—walls, floor, piles of what must have been furniture and books. Holes in the walls, the floor. A huge hole in the ceiling, through which I could see the white afternoon sky. The only snap of color was a red metal ladder standing in the corner. Balanced upon the ladder was a person who was neither Angus nor Deputy Chief Huntington, but a guy poking around what looked to be an attic space. A guy in his twenties, cussing to himself, mad as spit.

- 7 -

"Hello? Hi there, I–"

The guy's head snapped around. Like that girl in your class who's created a whole personality around being scared of spiders and bugs, he shrieked, high and loud. He wore work boots, jean cutoffs, and an old red-and-brown flannel work shirt with the sleeves hacked off. Threads dangled beneath his armpits. He had huge muttonchop sideburns that stuck out from the sides of his face and thick aviator glasses. His face was red and sweaty. "Who are you? What do you want?"

"I'm a friend of Angus's. I was supposed to meet him—"

"He's not here! Does he look like he's here? That little twerp. You just about gave me a heart attack. And after all that's gone down around here lately, that's the last thing I need, believe you me." He poked his head into the attic space and thrust his arms up there, too. He grunted with the effort of reaching, then pulled down a green metal file box. He set the box on the top step of the ladder before climbing down.

"I'm Minerva Clark." I stepped forward and offered my hand. It was a trick I'd learned—if you want someone to tell you their name, give them yours first.

"Wade. Wade Leeds," he said, without shaking my hand. He was too busy moving the file box from the ladder to the floor. So this was Wade, the grandson of the lady Angus called Grams, the poor lady who had died up here. I tried not to think about it. I watched Wade kneel beside the box. He struggled to open its tiny latch. The lid creaked open. I peeked over his shoulder. It looked as if it were full of school papers, cards made out of construction paper and glitter. Suddenly, he bent his head and started sobbing.

Can I just say . . . awkward!

Had I ever seen a grown man cry? I tried to remember whether there was something special you were supposed to do, like CPR, only for a man crying jag.

"I'm sorry about your grandma," I said to Wade Leeds. I took a step toward him.

Just as abruptly as he'd started weeping, he stopped. He snuffled loudly, blew his nose into his fingers, wiped them on his shirt, and stood up.

"Who you talking about?"

"Uh, your Grams?" I said. *Please*, I prayed, *do NOT make me say, "You know, who burned to death in the fire."*

"You mean my *ma*? Who was a good woman who never hurt a soul in her entire life? It's that Angus, he and his snot-nosed friends called her Grams, but she was hardly old. She was forty-seven. Her hair . . . ," his voice wobbled, ". . . her hair was prematurely white. That's all. She was a beautiful woman, a beautiful soul. I bet that twerp didn't tell you she cooked for the homeless, did he? Every Wednesday night for seventeen years. She painted, too. Watercolors."

"I'm really sorry," I said.

"This is all that's left," he said, shutting the file box. "This is it. Finito."

"But maybe . . . well . . . isn't there always a will or something?"

He picked up the box by its skinny wire handle and started toward the door. He stopped once and looked around the place, at the charred walls, the broken windows. He squinted up at the hole in the ceiling. "Ha, yeah, a will. Sure thing. A lady who cooks every week for the homeless has a will. Try debts. Up to her sweet ol' eyeballs."

I followed him back down the narrow staircase, through the grocery, and out onto the sidewalk. I waited while he replaced the padlock. "If you're looking for Angus, I ain't seen him," he growled.

"Where were you when the fire broke out?" I blurted out.

He turned and glared at me through his thick glasses. "Not where I shoulda been, which is home making sure Ma got out okay, now, was I?"

Around the corner from the grocery, parked beneath the shade of a huge Hawthorne tree, sat a dusty old Ford Explorer. A faded bumper sticker said, NOBODY DIED WHEN CLINTON LIED. Through the back window I could see a pile of stuff—some clothes and shoes, a box of groceries, some empty two-liter soda bottles, a sleeping bag, and a pillow with a dirty flowered case.

I watched stupidly while Wade Leeds unlocked the car door and stuffed a pile of shirts into the back. He put the green metal file box on the passenger seat next to a shaving kit. The zipper was open. Inside I could see one of those plastic travel boxes you keep soap in, a red-and-white can of shaving cream, a razor, and a hairbrush.

Before he slammed the car door and drove off, he said, "That Angus is bad news, and if you're a smart girl, you'll stay away."

Oooo-oooo-oooo-ahhnn! Thumpa-thumpa-thumpa. *Oooo-oooo-oooo-ahhnn!* Thumpa-thumpa-thumpa. Before answering the call, I watched Wade Leeds drive slowly to the end of the block. The rear bumper hung down on one side, making the vehicle and Wade Leeds look more pathetic than ever. I sighed and flipped open my phone.

"Where are you?" said Angus. He sounded mad. Mad! When he was the one who was an hour late.

"Huh? I'm here. Where are you?"

"Waiting for you."

"Where?" I looked up and down the street. Two houses down from the grocery a lady sat on her front porch smoking a cigarette and petting her cat. There was no other human activity that I could see.

"I'm here. At my house. Waiting for you, Minerva, intrepid goddess of warriors and poetry. Did you know Minerva invented music, too? I looked it up online. No wonder you rock."

"At your house?" I said. What was he talking about? I stared at the mural on the side of the grocery, at the snow-covered volcano spewing out tomatoes, zucchinis, and corn. When we'd talked the night before, I was sure we'd agreed to meet at the grocery.

"I'm a-waitin' for my wheels, too."

"Oh, right!" My meeting with Wade Leeds had been so bizarre I'd forgotten all about Angus's Go-Ped. I dashed back around the corner. It was still propped where I'd left it, against the garden wall across the street. I exhaled. That would have sucked if someone had stolen it.

Angus's house was six blocks away, straight down the tree-lined street. He lived in one of the old arty hippie houses. It was tall and skinny, and painted the color of a raspberry, with purple-and-cream-colored trim. The front yard was a lush garden of lavender and white roses and a bunch of other flowers I couldn't name.

A lady wearing faded jeans and a big straw hat knelt in the garden, working a trowel in the dark soil beneath one of the roses.

"Angus is inside," she said, looking up briefly.

This must be Angus's mom, I thought. She had the same dark eyes and freckles. I took a step forward, then stopped. "I'm sorry about your grocery," I said.

Then she smiled, and it was Angus's smile. "Why thank you. That's very sweet."

I steered the Go-Ped up onto the porch and tapped on the door.

Angus opened the door for me to enter. "I called Robotective and told him about that Paisley chick. He's going to look into it. He didn't say when or anything. Isn't there anything else we can do to nail her? We don't want her to strike again or anything."

I tripped over the doorstep, dragging the Go-Ped in with me. He didn't grab it from me, or tell me to leave it on the porch, or anything. As I passed him, I smelled his Old Spice aftershave. For some reason, it made me want to giggle. Angus was an oddball, and I don't just mean the trench-coat wearing in the dead of summer. There was something else, something I couldn't put my finger on.

He sauntered into the living room. It was cool and dark. Nat and Nat must have had air-conditioning.

The red walls were plastered with black-and-white photographs of people with lots of long hair, big grins, and a lot of beaded necklaces. In some of them I recognized the lady gardening in the front yard. Angus dropped onto the couch. The springs creaked.

I stood in the entryway, still holding his Go-Ped by the handlebars.

"Oh right," he said. "Just stick that over by the coat-rack thing."

"Thanks for letting me borrow it," I said.

"No worries. I've got another one," he said.

"I thought you were so hot to get this one back," I said.

"I was hot to see you," he said.

"Uh-huh," I said. I hoped it sounded cool. Maybe that's why he struck me as weird. I'd never had some-one madly in love with me before. Kevin liked me, but not in a desperate way that caused people to hatch plots and order beheadings, like in long-ago England. Maybe that's where Angus had found himself. Desperately in love with Minerva Clark, whom he'd contacted one day to help him solve a mystery. Now he found himself in over his head.

"Anyway, the other one's broken," he said, and then he laughed. He flipped on the TV, a flat-screen plasma job, sitting in the corner by a spidery tree in a green ce-ramic pot.

"Can I wash my hands or something?" They were

sticky from the snickerdoodle, and I wanted a minute to figure out how to break the news to him that our number one suspect was no suspect at all. He directed me to the kitchen, at the back of the house. After I washed my hands, I searched around for a towel and spied a stack of orange-striped ones folded in a pile atop a metal rack in the mudroom. I grabbed one, and as I dried my hands, I noticed there was a mangled-looking bag of Only Ferrets ferret food in one corner.

"Do you have a ferret?" I asked as I came back into the living room. He pressed the Mute on the remote.

"No, but I'd like one. We babysat a friend's ferret for a week while they went on vacation. They are such cool little creatures."

"Listen, we've got to talk. I don't think Paisley set the fire," I said.

"Just because we don't have any evidence yet? That's typical of arson, isn't it? The evidence gets burned up in the fire."

"Have you ever met Paisley?" I asked.

His gaze shifted to the TV screen. A science program was on. A man with a British accent was talking about coral reefs. "Don't think so. Maybe."

"She said she's a good friend of your aunt Maureen's."

Angus stared at the screen and pulled on his bottom lip. I figured out what his eyes reminded me of—chocolate M&M's. "They're all dying off, the coral reefs. It's because the ocean has heated up. All's it takes is, like, one degree, and there go all the coral. They bake to death."

"Paisley said she was the first person outside your family to hold you after you were born."

"Really?" The lopsided grin, the chipped front tooth. "Did it rock her world?"

"Like you need to ask?" I could play this game, too. I sat down on the other end of the couch. It was cushy and cool on my legs. I could have curled up and taken a nap.

"I might have met her," he said. "After she'd held me as a baby and all, but I gotta tell you, all my aunt Maureen's friends look alike."

"You'd remember Paisley. She's in a wheelchair." I remembered Paisley's curled pink hands, her perfect polished nails.

I let this information soak in. On the television, purple sea fans waved drowsily at us from their tropical ocean home.

"Yeah, so?" said Angus.

"So," I said, "I'm not sure she could have set a fire, even if she'd wanted to. And I doubt she wanted to, since your mom and dad were giving her the space in the grocery for free."

"Just because someone has a disability doesn't mean they're incapable of arson," he said. His tone was that of a stern grandpa.

"What are you *talking* about?" I said.

"It's not cool to discriminate against people like that," he said.

"Wait, *you're* the one who made fun of Detective Huntington's Eye of Doom."

"I'm mocking. That's different from discriminating."

Suddenly, the room didn't feel as cool as it had when I'd walked in. The air smelled stale. Talking to Angus was like trying to stand on an air mattress in a swimming pool. Just when you thought you had your balance, over you'd go into the drink. I thought about what Wade had said about Angus being bad news.

"She could have been faking it," he said.

"The wheelchair? She was not faking the wheelchair." This was truly beginning to bug me. I flipped open my phone to check the time. "Look . . . ," I said. "It's not Paisley, all right?"

"You're not giving up, are you?" he asked suddenly. I didn't think Angus was a mind reader, but he did always seem to say just what I was thinking two seconds before I was able to formulate the thought. Was I giving up? "That newspaper story about you made it sound like you weren't a quitter. You're not a quitter, are you?"

"I don't know," I said. I couldn't think of one reason why I shouldn't quit. Other than that I wanted a mystery to solve. Mrs. Dagnitz was probably home by now, pitching a fit about Morgan and me skipping out on her dumb yoga class. I'd been to a yoga class once, with one of Mark Clark's girlfriends, and it had made me all noodle-y and lazy. Why it didn't have this effect on my mother was probably a better mystery to be solving than this one.

"What about Wade Leeds?" I asked. I so totally did not think it was Wade Leeds—He Who Lived in His Car—but the idea of going back out into the afternoon heat and trying to figure out what bus would get me home, where I would get GOT for sure, made me want to pretend I thought it was him, just so I wouldn't have to move. I felt my eyes drift close.

"Wade. That weird dude. I never thought of him!" said Angus. "I bet it was him. He's a total freak." Angus was so enthusiastic I opened my eyes and glanced over at him. He was joking, right?

"It was not Wade Leeds," I said. I told him about the whole weird event, finding him looking in the attic for the file box, and him sobbing, and seeing all the stuff in his car.

"That Explorer belonged to Grams," said Angus.

"Who wasn't his grandma, but his mother, FYI," I said.

"Really? Weird."

"And no will. I asked him."

"Maybe he was lying," said Angus.

"He wasn't lying," I said.

We sat there for a few minutes. I felt myself dozing off again. Suddenly, I heard the squeaky springs on the couch again and got a whiff of Angus's Old Spice. He'd moved over closer to me on the couch. He put his hand gently on the back of my head, where it rested against the cushion. I stared into his chocolate M&M's eyes, and then he moved in for a kiss.

I had now been officially kissed by two boys, and I was only going into eighth grade, and I did not have straight swingy hair or a closet full of Juicy Couture. Not bad, huh? We opened our eyes, and I said, "I have a boyfriend, you know."

"I know," he said.

"You do? Did I ever tell you?"

"How could you not have a bf? You're so incredibly awesome."

"Well, thanks," I said. "You're incredibly awesome, too." It only seemed polite to say that back, even though I didn't quite mean it the way Angus did. I meant it more like the old-fashioned meaning of "awesome," as in "I'm in awe at how weird you are."

"Look," he said, playing with my hair, "it's okay if you think we've reached a dead end here."

"It is?" Only moments ago, he'd basically said I was a quitter.

"Of course. I totally trust your expertise. But would you do me one favor?"

"What?"

"Stop by the grocery on your way home and just have one last look around. I at least want to think I tried to help Nat and Nat."

"How do I get in?"

He laughed. That chipped front tooth. "That padlock doesn't need a key. It only looks locked. Just pull down on it."

I left Angus's air-conditioned raspberry-colored hippie house, passing his mom, still on her knees in the garden. She didn't see me go. I walked back down Southwest Corbett Avenue, just the way I'd come. I headed for the grocery. Of course I did. Angus Paine had kissed me. I wasn't *into* Angus Paine, but I still liked knowing he was into me. He thought I was incredibly awesome. I picked a daisy from someone's raggedy parking-strip garden and stuck it behind my ear. La la la. It fell out immediately, then I stepped on it.

I moseyed along. My feet were sweating so much inside my Chucks, I feared you could smell them from the outside. Maybe Mrs. Dagnitz was right about venturing into the world of shoes, or at least the world of sandals. I should have asked Angus for a cool drink of water before I left. I thought about Jupiter, snoozing in the cool basement at home. I hoped he had enough water. It's very easy for ferrets to die of dehydration. I texted Kevin and told him that Angus Paine was a freak who wore Old Spice. He told me about taking Harvey and Otis to get tacos for lunch and finding a Band-Aid in his enchilada. All of a sudden, I was so glad to have Kevin as my boyfriend.

I called Mark Clark on his cell and weirdly, I was not

on the verge of getting GOT until Christmas. He'd gone to lunch and to run some errands with Mr. and Mrs. Dagnitz and they'd just walked in the door. He thanked me for cleaning up the TP without him having to ask.

"Are you all right?" I asked. "You sound wiped."

"I am wiped." One of the errands had involved going to four different stores to find him a suitable suit for the Wedding Reception of the Century, as Quills called it, now only three days away.

"Suitable suit, ha ha ha," I said.

"Shut up, Minerva," said Mark Clark.

At the grocery, I gave the padlock a tug, just as Angus had instructed, and the shackle slid open easy as you please. I closed the charred door behind me. I didn't know what I was supposed to be looking for here. I found a piece of wood in a corner and poked through some of the debris. Aside from some half-burned potato-chip bags, I couldn't identify much of anything. I walked around the empty deli case and stepped over some scorched floorboards. How nice it would be to find an arson note: "I burned down this grocery because they stopped selling my favorite kind of red licorice. Signed, Lunatic Down the Block."

I sighed, planted myself in the middle of the store for a long minute, and looked around just because I couldn't think of anything else to do.

Suddenly, there was an odd sound—a cross between

a squeak and a click. *Squweeker. Squweeker-squweeker-squweeker.* It sounded like a cartoon mouse jumping on a trampoline, or no, that wasn't quite it . . .

The first noise was joined by a second one. Now it was a duet. *Sqweeker-squweeker-squweeker.* The sound was coming from inside. More squeaky clicks joined by what sounded like a wind-up monkey banging his tiny cymbals together. What was going on?

I spun around. Out of the corner of my eye I glimpsed something moving atop the shelf that held the antique toaster collection.

The levers on the ends of the toasters were going up and down, up and down, all by themselves.

The chrome-plated doors of the older toasters fell open, then slammed shut, making that strange cymbal noise. What the heck? A thought appeared that I couldn't shake—where were Mrs. Potts and Lumiere, the teapot and the candelabra from *Beauty and the Beast*?

I didn't think to get scared until the handle of the walk-in freezer clicked down and the freezer door slowly opened.

How could I have forgotten the ghost?

– 8 –

When I walked in the back door, Mrs. Dagnitz was standing in the middle of the kitchen with her hands on her hips, saying, "Why does it still smell like fish in here?" She had that crease between her forehead. Everyone was in their normal places. Mark Clark was in front of the computer. Quills was in the basement practicing his bass. Morgan was in his room reading.

She was talking to Quills, Mrs. Dagnitz was. He'd come upstairs for a Mountain Dew. He was tapping out a rhythm on the top of the can with two fingers, still listening to some inner tune. For a split second, I felt a little bad for Mrs. Dagnitz. Really, no one listened to her. When you're a mom who follows your yoga instructor to another state, no one listens to you.

She was right. The entire bottom floor of Casa Clark

reeked. I'd noticed it the second I'd opened the door. The smell was gross enough to interrupt my nonstop freak-out at having survived a paranormal experience. That's what it was called, right? When you caught a ghost acting up? I'd already called Reggie from the bus. Wasn't there, or wasn't picking up. Then I'd tried to call Kevin. Wasn't there, or wasn't picking up. Then I'd tried to call Angus. Went straight to voice mail.

All the way home on the bus my thoughts had ricocheted around my head. I had seen all those toaster levers sliding up and down with my own eyes. I had seen the freezer door swinging open with my own eyes. I had been alone in the grocery.

I chewed my cuticles, as nasty a habit as nail-biting, but I didn't care.

It had to have been Louise, the ghost in the walk-in, the Kikimora. Except it couldn't be Louise, the Kikimora. No person with half a brain believed in ghosts. It was like believing in unicorns, the Loch Ness monster, Big Foot, special personal angels who watched over you. I calmed down thinking of all the lame woo-woo things that did not exist, ghosts included.

Then how did you explain the toasters pretending to be toasting and ejecting their invisible pieces of toast? How did you explain the door of the walk-in freezer opening all on its own? The door had been shut firmly—I'd heard the smart click of the handle as clearly as Mrs. Dagnitz's voice complaining about the fish smell.

"That halibut was fresh," she said. "It shouldn't smell like this. Minerva, don't you smell it?"

"It's disgusting," I said, pinching my nose shut with my fingers.

Quills shrugged and took his opportunity to slink back down into the basement.

I was happy to help Mrs. Dagnitz throw open the windows and reclean the counters with Windex, grateful not to be in trouble for having missed family yoga that morning.

"Don't go easy on the stuff," she said over my shoulder. "We have got to get that smell out of here before I do something I regret."

"Like order a bag of McDonald's fries? They cover every smell in the world. They've done wonders for the inside of Quills's car."

Mrs. Dagnitz laughed. "Really? I just might have to try that."

I knew she never would. Mickey D's excellent fries had nothing in common with broccoli or pomegranate juice or any other antioxidant food. Still, she didn't get all horrified over my admitting I had firsthand knowledge of McDonald's, and after I was finished scrubbing the counters, she let me go.

Before heading up to my room I trotted down to the basement and plucked Jupiter from where he snoozed in his hammock on the third floor of Ferret Tower. I cradled him in the crook of my arm like a baby doll. He blinked and trembled a little, his usual behavior before he's fully awake and eager to hide your shoes. The moment I let Jupiter loose in my room, he did his mad ferret inchworm dance straight under a pile of dirty clothes.

Out of habit, I took my rebus notebook from my desk drawer—a composition notebook with a purple-and-white marble cover. I sat down in front of my computer and IMed Reggie, who you can find online pretty much around the clock, especially since he'd been dumped by his first real girlfriend, Amanda the Panda, a ballet dancer one grade ahead of us.

Ferretluver: Hey Reg. Here's a rebus for you: **Noon lazy**.
BorntobeBored: D'oh. Lazy afternoon. You're losing your touch, Minerva C.
Ferretluver: Yeah well, I'm a little distracted these days.
BorntobeBored: Breaking up with the tool?
Ferretluver: You mean Kevin? Just cuz you got kicked to the curb by the Panda that's no reason to be Regzilla.
BorntobeBored: Been tortured by more wedding shopping?
Ferretluver: It's just a reception. They already got married.
BorntobeBored: Whatevah.

Ferretluver: So I gotta ghost question.
BorntobeBored: Mwahhahahaha.
Ferretluver: Do you think a ghost could set a fire?
BorntobeBored: Duh.
Ferretluver: Duh? Like this happens all the time?
BorntobeBored: Just saw a cool TV show on a haunted jail, where a guy who died in one of the cells used to set the beds on fire. Every prisoner they ever stuck in there burned to a crisp while he slept. Which turned THEM into ghosts. So now the jail cell is doubly haunted.
Ferretluver: Riiiiiiight. Thank you. Drive through, please.
BorntobeBored: I'm not being The Exaggerator!

The Exaggerator was Reg's superhero identity—he said if he ever was called upon to rid the world of evil, he wouldn't lift a sword, but would force the evildoers to surrender by exaggerating everything he said until they begged for mercy.

We joked about that for a while. Then he said that in his humble opinion an unexplained fire was actually a ghost temper tantrum. He said that really old places like Ireland have a lot of cranky temper-tantrum-throwing ghosts, and that every pub and church had a story about a fire being set in it. Then he logged off to watch a documentary about King Tut.

Kevin popped on for a while and IMed me about his

cousin visiting from Vacaville, California, and about his new World of Warcraft character. We had been boyfriend and girlfriend for two weeks. Some of my friends had one boyfriend in the morning, but another one by the afternoon. By comparison, Kevin and I were like an old married couple. His new character was a gnome rogue, MiniVanDamme, specializing in assassination and leather-working. I wondered if IMing him about MiniVanDamme was the same as watching him play WoW, something I vowed I would never, ever do.

While I was IMing with Kevin, Angus called my cell and I let it go to voice mail.

His message said, "You must be tired—you've been running through my head all day long." This was a well-known lame-o flirt line, but I couldn't tell by Angus's tone of voice whether he was using it for real or not.

For some reason I couldn't name, I decided I didn't want to talk to Angus just yet. Even though I'd tried to call him the second after I'd torn out of the grocery—the toaster levers hopping up and down behind me, the door to the walk-in freezer swung open wide—now that I'd calmed down, something told me to wait, to collect my thoughts, to figure out a few things.

I couldn't get the idea of a ghost temper tantrum out of my head. I didn't know much about ghosts, but it stood to reason that if they were so difficult that they refused to move on to the higher plane, they would be prone toward pitching hysterical fits. I Googled

"Kikimora," half hoping my search would return the name of a band or an anime character, but there it was: "Kikimora is a female house spirit in Slavic mythology."

Angus was telling the truth.

The average Kikimora is a small humpbacked woman in a tattered dress. She usually lives behind the stove or in the basement (or in a walk-in freezer!!), and minds her own business as long as her home is not disturbed. If someone fails to keep her home tidy or if it is disturbed in any way, she grows enraged. Reading this, I could feel the blood thrumming inside my head. I tried to remember my conversation with Paisley. Had she said they were rearranging anything in the grocery to make way for her pastry counter? The grocery wasn't large, so Nat and Nat *must* have moved some stuff around.

Then I read this: "Once angered, the Kikimora will come out of her hiding place and spin. If a person witnesses a Kikimora spinning, they will soon die."

I leaped up from my desk, knocking my chair over, sprinted to the end of the third-floor hall, and took the fire pole straight down into the kitchen, startling Mark Clark, who was starting the dishwasher.

"You haven't done that in a while," said Mark Clark.

"What?" I cried. I wondered if watching old toasters toast ghostly slices of bread was somehow the same as spinning.

"Taken the pole. You said you were too old for it."

"I took it just a couple days ago," I said. Who cares when I last took the pole! I was possibly on the verge of death. It didn't say how the person witnessing the spinning Kikimora died. Did their blood turn to sand? Did they spontaneously combust? Were they hit by a truck?

Mark Clark pressed the Start button and the dishwasher started making its swooshy-swishy cleaning sound. "When you were a baby, you had this portable crib, and if you had trouble sleeping, we'd roll you in here and start up the dishwasher, even if there weren't any dishes in it. You'd fall asleep in a second."

"How cute of me!" I said. I was panting. I collected my hair, tied it in a big knot on top of my head, and then pulled it out again.

"Are you all right?" he asked.

"It still smells like fish in here," I said. "Why does it still smell like fish?" I sounded like Mrs. Dagnitz, obsessing about the fish odor. Maybe this was my mother's problem—she'd seen a Kikimora spinning there among the ancient Indian pueblos of Santa Fe and was on edge from awaiting her death. Morgan was right. I should be nicer.

I tried to catch my breath, told myself that it would be all right, that I had not seen Louise spinning, nor had I seen Louise at all. And if worse came to worst, and I had seen her spinning, ideally I would die before Saturday, which would mean I wouldn't have to go to Mrs. Dagnitz's wedding reception.

Mark Clark and I got ourselves Otter Pops, then watched a movie on his monitor. The computer room was the coolest place in the house because it had what is called a cross breeze. The movie was PG-13. There was some smooching and some jokes that I didn't get that made Mark Clark grimace and go, "Aw no," then reach over and cover my ears with his palms. I'd forgotten all about Jupiter, rummaging around upstairs in my room. I did not want to go back up there by myself, but if I asked Mark Clark to come with, he'd wonder why, and I wasn't into having a don't-be-silly-there's-no-such-thing-as-ghosts lecture.

Lucky for me, when I raced back upstairs, Jupiter was curled up inside a bucket hat I'd left on the floor, sound asleep.

In the morning, after I'd eaten a bowl of muesli (yuck!) and a container of strawberry yogurt, I called Mrs. Dagnitz and asked her if she needed me to do anything for Mark Clark's birthday, which we were celebrating that night. Did she want me to clean the dining room? Bake Mark Clark's favorite yellow cake with mocha frosting?

"Does the kitchen still smell like fish?" she asked.

The kitchen did still smell like fish. The entire bottom floor still smelled like fish. When Quills had come home the previous night from listening to some music somewhere, he'd said, "Gawd, did Shamu die in here or something?"

"Kinda," I said.

"I don't think I can possibly cook in that kitchen with this heat and that fish smell," said Mrs. Dagnitz. "That halibut was—"

"Fresh. I know," I said. "We practically caught it ourselves. I'll Windex the counters again. Should I scrub the floor, too?"

To my ears I sounded like a total poseur, but my tactic worked. Mrs. Dagnitz said I didn't need to do that. It was so thoughtful of me to offer to help, but she had it all under control and I should go out and enjoy my summer and realize that these were the best years of my life. She asked if I was going to see that lovely friend Chelsea, and I lied and said of course, that Chelsea and I were practically inseparable and that today we were going to practice new hairdos and paint our nails and go to the mall and shop for accessories.

"Just make sure you're home by, say, five o'clock."

"I'll call you from my cell when I'm leaving Chelsea's," I said.

Sometimes I was such a good daughter.

Cryptkeeper Ron's real name was Ron Freary. He owned a car dealership near the mall that sold—well, I wasn't sure what kind of cars they were. It took no sleuthing at all to find this information. Watch late-night television for more than ten minutes and you will be assaulted by a "Come to Ron Freary's for a Scary Good

Deal" commercial. Quills always joked that the scary thing about Ron Freary was not his deals, but the cornflake-sized pieces of dandruff clinging to the shoulders of his sports coat.

Morgan let me borrow his mountain bike. I caught him just as he was walking out the door with poor Ned, corgi and babe magnet. "Say 'hey' to Jeannette for me!" I called as I swooshed down the driveway. Out of the corner of my eye I could see him frowning after me.

If anyone would know about Louise, and whether she was capable of setting a fire, it would be Cryptkeeper Ron. It was because of her that he'd put Corbett Street Grocery on his tour of haunted Portland.

As I coasted down through the neighborhoods, I tried hard to remember going on the Halloween tour. It had been more than two years ago. Practically another lifetime. We'd bombed around town in a bus painted black, with a waving ghost painted on the side.

We stopped at an apartment house, a boarded-up factory that made Styrofoam heads for wigs and hats, and at a cemetery that should have been way scary, but it was across the street from a burger joint broadcasting the World Series, and as we tromped around the gravestones you could hear guys hollering, "Hey, Ump! One more eye and you'd be a Cyclops!"

The grand finale was a maze of the narrow tunnels

that ran beneath a local tavern, where in times of yore sailors were shanghaied, drugged and kidnapped, and stuck on an oceangoing ship, where they were forced to work as crew members. Cryptkeeper Ron said that even some stragglers touring the tunnels had gone missing, but that his lawyers told him never to mention that. Har! I was in fifth grade, and even I'd known it was a joke. I remember touching one of the tunnel walls. It was wet, even though there was no water anywhere that I could see. That frightened me more than any talk of shanghaied sailors.

My brothers liked the tour because they thought I had more fun than I did. Afterward, we went out for dessert and I ate chocolate mousse for the first time.

I had not expected Cryptkeeper Ron to be strolling around his dealership in the midday sun, hands in his pockets, just like any salesman on the job. Despite the balloons and banners announcing a sale, no one was interested in buying a car today. You could fry many things on the hoods of those shiny new cars.

"What can I do for you today, little lady? Daddy promise you a new car when you get your license?"

I wore a pair of baggy plaid shorts, a white tank top, and my red-and-blue Chucks with the white skulls on the ankles. My curly/wavy hair snarled around my head from the bike ride, and my cuticles were raw from the previous day's gnaw-fest.

Did I really look like a girl whose "Daddy" would buy

her a car when she turned sixteen? Did I look fifteen and a half? It was the five-eight talking. People saw tall and they thought older.

"He always says he wants to get me a Volvo, but I really like . . ." I glanced around the lot. What kind of cars were these anyway? Then I glimpsed the huge white letters across the front of the showroom—Hyundai. How did you pronounce this car? ". . . I've always wanted a Hunday." I tried to iron the question mark out of the end of that sentence. Yes, that's right. I've always wanted a Hunday.

"Can't blame you there. Nope, no ma'am and no sir."

Cryptkeeper Ron—for that is the only way I could think of him—showed me a purple Hyundai with leather upholstery, power steering, antilock brakes, and a bunch of other stuff. He mentioned crash-dummy tests and statistics and warranties. He was eager for me to call Daddy and drag him down here pronto so we could go over some figures.

This was not turning out the way I wanted it to.

"Actually, to be totally honest? The real reason I want a Hunday is because I am a huge fan of your haunted Portland tour."

He grinned and hung his thumbs inside his waistband. "You like my tour, eh?"

"My brothers took me when I was in fifth grade. I thought it was so awesome."

"Really now. You should get them to take you again.

I've added a few new locales. An old warehouse in the Pearl, got a ghost in the freight elevator."

"Freight elevator! That reminds me of my favorite ghost—in the walk-in freezer at that grocery store."

"Oh yes, that presence is a strong one," said Cryptkeeper Ron. He tipped back on his heels and nodded.

"A strong one. Does that mean, like, an extra-bad ghost?" I asked.

"It means her vibrations are very easy to detect," said Cryptkeeper Ron. His gaze wandered around the lot. He pulled a handkerchief out of his back pocket and blotted his forehead. He was hot and losing interest.

"I thought that of all the ghosts, that one seemed the most real because, like, there's nothing obviously creepy or moody about a grocery store. Not like an old church, or those tunnels. Those are kind of obvious ghostly haunts."

"Obvious?" said Cryptkeeper Ron. "What are you saying? There are stops on the tour that are too obvious?"

"No . . . ," I said lamely.

Cryptkeeper Ron was sure prickly. I didn't remember his comb-over in fifth grade. I could see his pink scalp shining with sweat beneath gauzy threads of graying blond hair.

"Not many folks like the Corbett Grocery. Feel it's too tame. Not spooky enough. In fact, I've thought about dumping 'em, but they've been part of the tour since day one. Kinda don't have the heart. Know what I mean? They're good people, Nat and Nat."

"That means you must know my friend Angus."

"Him!" Cryptkeeper Ron snorted, then caught himself up. He was a businessman after all. He couldn't just go around randomly rolling his eyes. "He was a cute little kid. Really a smart little guy. He was just a ball to have around. When he was a little kid. So!" He clapped his hands, obviously finished with the conversation. "Let's see what we can do to get you into a nice little Excel. What did you say your name was?"

"Minerva Clark." I put out my hand.

He took my hand and shook it, staring hard at me all the while. Then he snapped his fingers and wagged his finger at me. "I know you. How do I know you? Your folks bought from me before?"

Was this more salesman patter? How would I know how he knew me? "Does one of your kids go to Holy Family? That's where I go and—"

"The newspaper. You're that kid who thinks she's the new Magnum P.I."

"Who?"

"Get outta here," he said. He tucked his head and made that shooing gesture usually saved for bad cats hogging the furniture.

"Excuse me?"

"Get lost! Shoo. I don't want you on my property. I don't know why you're here, or what you're quote unquote investigating, but I don't want you around."

"I'm really just interested in the ghost at Corbett Street Grocery."

"There is no ghost at Corbett Street Grocery, all rightie? Now scat!"

Cryptkeeper Ron lies.

- 9 -

I rode home in the afternoon heat, trying to figure out what had gone wrong in my conversation with Cryptkeeper Ron. Since my accident, I'd been able to read people pretty well. But I'd read Ron Freary all wrong. Like with a complicated algebra equation I'd forgotten to factor in something, in this case the newspaper profile. The same story that encouraged Angus Paine to ask me to help him solve his mystery made Cryptkeeper Ron suspicious.

I was deep in pondering as I swerved into our driveway, past Mrs. Dagnitz's white Pathfinder. The back door of Casa Clark was wide open. I could smell the rotten fish smell outside. *Outside*. This wasn't good.

In the kitchen, Mrs. Dagnitz was saying, "Something must be dead in one of the cupboards. This can't simply be the fish after all this time. It was fresh fish!"

Weird Rolando was moving things out of the broom

closet—Ned's big bag of dog food, the mop, broom, and dustpan—and not finding anything. His hair was in a bun today. "Nothing in here, Buttercup."

I turned toward the dishwasher to hide my full-strength eye roll. Unloading the dishwater was one of my chores. As I pulled open the top rack, I noticed that the tiny ponds of water pooled in the bottom of the upside-down coffee cups and glasses was yellowish green. I had never seen an actual swamp, except on one of Mark Clark's video games, but that's what came to mind.

When I pulled the bottom rack out, I saw an entire lake of swamp-colored water in the bottom of the dish-washer. When I leaned down to pull out a bowl, I got a big whiff of fish smell.

"Ugh! Check this out," I said.

Mrs. Dagnitz and Weird Rolando gathered around the dishwasher and peered inside.

"Oh God!" said Mrs. Dagnitz. "Something's plugged. The thing's not draining. Are those the dishes from when we had the fish? They are! Why didn't we wash them sooner? What are they doing still sitting in there?"

"Maybe we can get a plumber out before the end of the day," said Weird Rolando.

"I doubt it," said Mrs. Dagnitz. "This is just great. I cannot cook in this kitchen. I simply cannot cook in this kitchen. I knew I should have listened to my inner voice and booked a private room at Blue Hour."

Mrs. Dagnitz needed some yoga in the worst way. I

stood there with a fish-juice-coated bowl in my hands. "But Mom, even if we would have run the dishwasher a day earlier, it still wouldn't have drained properly."

Mark Clark, known from now on as Mr. Terrible Timing, picked that moment to walk through the door singing some cringe-worthy disco song he'd obviously just been playing in his car. You could tell by the bounce in his step that he expected to come home to a homemade cake and a nice lasagna baking in the oven. Even though it was eight thousand degrees, and the only dinner that made any sense was Otter Pops.

Mrs. Dagnitz wheeled around and said, "Mark! Tell me you're running the dishwasher every day. You've got to run it every day, especially in the summer. It's not hygienic. I don't want to get a phone call that you're all dead out here from salmonella."

"We run it when it's full. To, you know, conserve water."

"Great," said Mrs. Dagnitz. "That's just great."

Mark Clark and I traded looks.

"Let me see what I can do," said Mark Clark. Back through the door he went.

"What should I do with the dishes?" I asked.

"Well, obviously we can't eat off of them, can we?" Mrs. Dagnitz cried. Weird Rolando slid behind her and started rubbing her shoulders. "It'll be okay, Buttercup."

Mark Clark returned with a coil of green garden

hose. He kept it in the trunk of his car in case he ever ran out of gas and needed to borrow some from another car. It wasn't exactly legal, but he only ever siphoned enough to get to the next gas station.

He uncoiled the hose and stuck one end in fish-juice lake. Then he leaned over the sink and started sucking on the other end.

"What are you doing!" shrieked our mother.

The kitchen now smelled like old fish and gasoline. My stomach tossed and turned. I held my nose. Mark Clark stuck his finger inside his mouth, pressed the top of the hose closed, then pulled the hose from his mouth and pointed the end into the sink. When he pulled his finger away, a stream of old fish water splashed down the drain.

At the same time, Mark Clark spit into the sink. He'd managed to swallow some of the old fish water.

"This is completely unacceptable. Where is your father? Does he know this sort of thing goes on?"

"St. Louis," I said.

"Or are you just doing this to spite me? To prove what a wretched mother I am for making the choices I did?"

"Or no, Cincinnati, I think. Last week he was in St. Louis."

"Don't do this to me," Mrs. Dagnitz sobbed.

Now she was crying. I watched Mark Clark patiently siphon the entire lake of old fish water into the sink.

Moments after he gave the sink a quick once-over with the Comet, the old-fish smell faded. Now the kitchen just smelled like gasoline.

At least Mrs. Dagnitz could start cooking. She didn't ask anybody to help. She was in one hundred percent martyr mode. You could probably see her pain and suffering from outer space. Weird Rolando and Mark Clark fetched some tools from the junk drawer and poked around the inside of the dishwasher and decided that, yes, a plumber needed to be called.

The plumber showed up just about the time . . .

. . . Mark Clark ran to the guest bathroom to puke his guts out. It was the combination of heat, old fish dishwasher water, and gasoline that did him in. Of all of us, Mark Clark's stomach is the most sensitive.

Quills got off work early—it was a slow day for photocopying and Kinko's sent him home—and hopped up and down with glee at the sight of the plumber, with his frizzy white hair and trademark sagging dirty jeans, sprawled beside the dishwasher, which he'd had to pull from beneath the counter.

"Cool! Innards. I loooovvvvvve innards!" Quills said, tugging on his spiky yellow hair.

Mrs. Dagnitz moved around the kitchen with her oven mitts, her nose literally in the air. She pretended as if he wasn't there.

"Hey, it doesn't smell like fish anymore!" Quills crowed.

"Michael, could you set the table, please?"

I couldn't help but giggle. Nobody called Quills Michael. Even his name tag from Kinko's said Quills.

Setting the table was my job, but I was getting the cold shoulder because I was the one who had found the lake of old fish water, and because I had pointed out that Charlie was in Cincinnati. Mrs. Dagnitz instructed *Michael* to use the linens (not the squares of paper towel we normally used for napkins), and to make sure we all had wineglasses. It wouldn't be a birthday dinner without a proper toast. Little did she know our traditional birthday toast was a song that went "Happy birthday / O happy birthday / Grief, misery, and despair, People dying everywhere! / O happy birthday / O happy birthday."

Then Mrs. Dagnitz dragged out a huge wooden salad bowl from the back of some cupboard—I don't think I'd ever seen it before—and filled it with a salad made of spinach (of course) and some weird lettuce that looked like weeds from the backyard. She pulled the lasagna from the oven, its cheese bubbly hot. Her thin blond hair was lank around her face, drenched with sweat. She looked hotter than anyone else in the room, and for some reason that made me feel guilty.

"Here's your problem," said the plumber. He held up a small piece of curved glass. It was the rim of one of our drinking glasses. "It was wedged in the filter, kept the water from draining out."

We stared at the shard of glass that had caused all the trouble. The plumber replaced a few hoses, reset the dishwasher in its square hole beneath the counter, and gave Weird Rolando a bill for two hundred dollars.

It could have been the amount of the plumber's bill that was the last straw, but I think it was Mark Clark throwing up that sent Mrs. Dagnitz over the edge. She picked up the piece of glass and held it out to me. "This is your fault."

"MY fault?"

"This is from a broken glass. You were obviously throwing a glass into the dishwasher and it broke."

"That was a long time ago," I said. "I told Mark Clark about it and he said it was an accident and we all have accidents and it was no big deal."

"No big deal. That's easy for him to say, isn't it? I've seen you load the dishwasher. You bang around listening to that iPod and don't pay the least attention. There's not a cereal bowl in this house that doesn't have a chip in it. I know you think that all the nice things you have just fall from the sky for your enjoyment, but this all costs money. I have half a mind to take this bill out of your allowance." She shook the plumber's bill in my face.

"I don't have an iPod," I said.

"Oh, for God's sake, Minerva, do you have to be contrary at every turn?"

"And I don't think it's easy for him to say."

"What?" she shrieked.

We glared at each other. I had that feeling you get on a roller coaster, when the car slowly powers uphill to that first huge drop, and it clanks along slowly, and you're feeling pent up and nervous because you know what's coming, and then there's that long moment when the car pauses at the top, and then the car tips forward and roars down the track and there's not one thing you can do but throw your hands into the hair and scream your head off.

"He's the one who's *here*," I snapped. "It's got to be much harder to put up with what a horrible monster I am when you're on the premises all the time."

"Are you saying I'm not here?" said Mrs. Dagnitz, her eyes so wide with disbelief I could see more white than blue.

Mrs. Dagnitz looked from Weird Rolando, who was grating some Parmesan cheese into a bowl, to Quills, who was at the sink filling a pitcher with water, to Morgan, who had just materialized from upstairs.

"Hey, the fish odor has dissipated," said Morgan.

No one said anything. We could hear Mark Clark behind the bathroom door, down the hall, coughing and moaning.

"But you're not here," I said. Was it really up to me, the almost fourteen-year-old, to point out the obvious?

"I'm here in spirit!" she wept, shoveling squares of

lasagna onto a plate. The steam rose from the glass casserole dish, making her cheeks even pinker. "Ask Rollie. All I think about is my family. You all mean everything to me, everything. You have no idea. I've had to make some very difficult decisions, which none of you can come close to appreciating. And then when I make the effort to come back to Portland to throw a party so that all of you can be included in my new life, you snub me."

As you know, I live in a house of boys. I live in a house of boys, and Reggie, my best friend, is a boy. If I had three sisters and a best friend who was a girl, I might have burst into tears myself, or thrown my arms around Mrs. Dagnitz and told her not to feel bad. Instead, the Louis Armstrong song that Quills and Mark Clark and Morgan always croon to one another when one of us is holding a personal pity party bubbled up from deep inside me. It's best if sung extra slowly, with your hand on your heart and your eyes rolled heavenward.

I sang, "Nobody knows the trouble I've seen . . ."

At that exact moment Mrs. Dagnitz had her spatula tucked under a square of lasagna. But instead of transferring it to a plate, she did the most amazing thing. If I had been able to stream it on the Internet, it would have made my mother famous. She cocked her arm back and hurled that piece of lasagna, with its steaming spinach and scalding tomato sauce and hot bubbly cheese, straight at my head. I am not the girl athlete my mother was—I recalled her telling me that when she was my age she played first base on an all-star softball team—but I'm quick. I ducked and threw my hands up. The blob of scalding lasagna grazed my forearm as it flew past, landing somewhere behind me, somewhere I was not about to clean up.

No one said anything. Then Quills said, "That wasn't very Zen of you, Mom."

That was the last thing I heard. I stomped outside, grabbed Morgan's bike, and sped off down the street.

The big question would become: Why did I go to Holy Family that night?

No one believed me that I always found myself there when life became a full-on stress-fest. Holy Family was K–8. This meant that instead of lush acres of green athletic fields where we middle schoolers could play soccer and flag football and have an idyllic puberty, there was a playground with holes for tetherball poles, a sandbox where stray dogs pooped during off-hours, and a huge teal-and-beige plastic play structure with a big plastic slide. Every eighth grader complained, but I secretly didn't mind the play structure. I liked to sit on the top of the slide and have deep thoughts.

I'd cried as I'd pedaled Morgan's bike from our house to the school, but by the time I dropped the bike in the bark dust, my mood had changed to plain old mean-mad-mean. Mrs. Dagnitz liked to think she was all honest and in touch and "authentic"—I hate that word!—but when you dared speak God's own truth around her, she threw a slab of scalding hot lasagna at your head. I examined my arm to see if perhaps some of the scalding cheese had given me a serious burn. Kevin knew a guy who'd had to go to the emergency room for burns to the roof of his mouth from digging into a piece of cheese pizza straight from the oven. I found a pale pink splotch near my elbow. It didn't look as if it was going to turn into the angry, oozing blisters I'd wanted to parade around at my mother's wedding reception. I imagined myself in my beautiful brown halter dress with the pink polka dots, sipping my 7Up from a crystal glass with my arm raised, my pinky stuck out all proper, and when people asked what happened to my arm, I could say, "The bride assaulted me with a square of scalding lasagna, thank you for asking."

I climbed up to the top of the slide and eased myself down, my legs thrust out straight in front of me. The sun had dipped behind a row of trees in the west, and the plastic was cool against my legs. The slide had a tall lip of plastic on either edge. I fit snuggly up there, like a toddler's puzzle piece pressed into the correct space. From my perch, I could see people entering and leaving the playground. A pair of giant teenage boys and their basketball, come to shoot some hoops. A tiny girl with an even tinier fluffy black-and-white puppy on a metallic red leash.

I waved to them all, and they all waved back.

I called Reggie to see if he would meet me for an IP, an in-person meeting. Years ago we'd agreed that IMing was for talking when you had nothing to say. When it was important, it had to be an IP. When Reggie didn't answer his cell, I tried his house. His dad said he was at his Reading Hieroglyphics class that night, and wouldn't be home until after ten.

Kevin's number was number two on my speed dial, after Reggie's. I suspected this meant something, but I didn't want to know what. I was finding out quickly that if you wanted to keep a boyfriend, you had to stop yourself from thinking about certain things. Sometimes I wonder if that's what happened with my mom and dad—one of them started thinking too much, and that led to divorce.

Kevin picked up after the first ring. "Yo!" I could hear a video game in the background, then a voice say, "I am so going to pwn you, dude!"

"I'm down at the school," I said, forgetting he didn't know about my habit of slide-sitting at Holy Family.

"Summer school?" he said. From years of watching my brothers play these stupid games I could tell that MiniVanDamme was now engaged in battle.

"My mother went insane today. She threw a piece of hot lasagna at me."

Long silence. I could hear another boy's voice murmuring in the background.

When Kevin didn't answer, I said, "I'm in the emergency room right now."

"Cool drop," he said to the other boy, but straight into his phone. "Is it better to have the extra agility or the extra armor?"

"They have to amputate my arm. Both arms, actually."

"That sucks," he said.

I pressed the End button, curious whether he'd call me back. I was beginning to doubt that we'd ever buy a ranch in Maui and raise Appaloosas.

At that moment, on the street that ran along the far end of the playground, I spied Daniel Vecchio and his posse of loathsome fifth graders, cruising the school on their bikes.

Oooo-oooo-oooo-ahhnn! Thumpa-thumpa-thumpa. *Oooo-oooo-oooo-ahhnn!*

I flipped open my phone. "Sometimes you can be a total jerk," I said, thinking it was Kevin calling back to apologize.

"I know, I know. That's why I've been trying to call you." It was Angus Paine, sounding genuinely wrecked.

I couldn't imagine why he thought I thought he was a jerk, but he said he felt crappy about when I came to his house, and how he practically called me a quitter, and doubted my conclusions about Paisley O'Toole and

Wade Leeds, and then hit on me when he knew I had a boyfriend, which was completely wrong, since he had total respect for me, and would never want to mess up my life.

I didn't think he'd been so rotten, and I told him so. I said I knew rude behavior, and he hadn't been rude at all. He kept insisting. "You've got to let me make it up to you," he said.

"But Angus, really, there's nothing to make up. You were totally cool."

We didn't talk any more about what he thought he'd done, but we did talk about everything else under the sun. I had never had a boy apologize to me for doing nothing before. We talked for 102 minutes, straight through Purpley Time and into the night.

I told him about stopping at the grocery on the way home from his house that day and having the bejesus scared out of me by the dancing toaster levers.

"That Louise," he said, as if she were a crazy aunt.

"Do you think . . . I know this sounds ridiculous . . . really ridiculous . . . but do you think maybe she set the fire? I mean, Kikimoras don't like it when their homes are disturbed, and maybe, with your parents rearranging the store so that Paisley could have her kiosk or whatever there, Louise felt threatened. I mean, if there really is a Louise. I don't really believe in ghosts or any of that woo-woo stuff, but . . . well . . . you know."

Angus Paine was silent for a long minute. I was used to this now, the way he clammed up for so long you thought the call had been dropped. "I'd totally believe it."

The streetlights came on. The only people left in the playground were the huge teenage boys shooting baskets. When the ball hit the rim, it made a low *clong* sound. After a while, the conversation spun down into random thoughts about our favorite YouTube videos, whether Green Day (my favorite band!) had sold out or not, and how lame our parents were. Unlike Kevin, Angus was interested to hear about how awful Mrs. Dagnitz's wedding reception was going to be. He asked when it was, and where it was, and whether I was expected to do anything totally embarrassing, like give a speech.

"Give a speech?" I croaked. I hadn't even thought of that.

"I have a friend whose dad did that, married someone else, and at the reception everyone had to say something about the couple. Something nice." He laughed.

We talked until my ear got hot from my cell phone. I did not want to go home, where I expected that another dramathon awaited me. Quills would be worried to death about where I'd been. You'd think it would be Mark Clark, who was usually the BIC, brother-in-charge, but he understood me better than the other brothers, and never lost his head. Morgan would have disappeared into his room, or maybe he'd met one of his friends for a game of cribbage, all the rage among philosophy students these days. I imagined Mrs. Dagnitz would be pacing around the living room, sobbing and twisting a shredded-up Kleenex in her strong hands, feeling so terrible that she'd assaulted her only daughter with her wholesome vegetarian cuisine.

But no.

When I finally got home, the kitchen was spotless, the fish smell long gone. Mrs. Dagnitz and Weird Rolando had returned to their hotel. Quills and Mark Clark were upstairs lounging on either ends of Cat Pee Couch watching a rerun of *The Simpsons*.

Quills patted the couch and I plopped down between them. Mark Clark put his arm around the back of the couch and patted my arm.

"You hanging out down at the school?" he asked.

I must have looked shocked that he knew my secret. "How'd you know?"

"Morgan saw ya when he was out walking the dog," said Mark Clark. "Plus, we all used to hide out down there. Must run in the family."

"Like the urge to throw burning Italian food at people?" I asked, all fake innocent.

Quills and Mark Clark glanced at each other and tried to look stern and older brotherly, but then Quills said in a fake judge voice, "Mrs. Rolando Dagnitz, the jury has found you guilty of assault with a deadly entrée," and we cracked up, and soon we were all wiping our eyes from laughing so hard. It was terrible. We should have had a somber and meaningful discussion, but we didn't. We couldn't.

– 10 –

I've been in deep trouble once or twice in my life, but I have never been in Maximum Trouble. Mount Everest is to the world's peaks what Maximum Trouble is to teenage bad behavior. Maximum Trouble involves punishment more serious than getting GOT. When you are in Maximum Trouble, people who were once on your side and thought you were cool change their way of thinking about you. Your parents and teachers are "disappointed" in you. Sometimes the law is involved. Also a special therapist for children.

After watching the rerun of *The Simpsons*—which I am usually not allowed to watch because Mark Clark thinks it's too raunchy—I washed my hair, checked Jupiter's food and water, and went to bed.

My biggest beauty secret is to go to bed with my hair soaking wet. Towel dry, finger-comb with whatever antifrizz product I find in the bathroom cabinet, then wad it up into a ball under my head. When I wake up in the morning? Perfect imperfect curly waves. In the summer it's almost as soothing as having an Otter Pop wrapped around my throat.

But on this night it was far from soothing. On this night I tossed and turned. My dreams were long and complicated and seemed to have a lot of sirens in them. Once, I awoke in the dark—had I been asleep for five minutes or five hours?—and the sirens sounded close enough to be in my room. It was also possible I was having a dream in which I woke up confused, thinking there were sirens in my room.

In the morning, my hair had dried to an impeccable mess, and there was drool on my pillow. I'd slept hard. I could tell by the light in my room that it was late. I poked my head out the windows over my desk. It was still warm, but the sky was a strange yellow gray. It smelled smoky, like people had been using their fireplaces. That was impossible, since fall was still months away.

I turned to see Quills standing in my bedroom door, tugging on a hunk of his crayon-yellow hair, his mouth a grim line. "Dude, you better get down there."

"Is Mrs. Dagnitz here, ready to throw an omelet at me or something?"

Quills just looked at me. It was as if we'd never made ourselves hysterical with our assault-with-a-deadly-entrée jokes the night before. Quills was two years younger than Mark Clark, but sometimes he seemed much younger. Morgan was more like Mark Clark—made tough by their serious view of the world—and Quills was more like me, the little sister with the wayward hair. He reminded me of a boy in my class who was six-three and had already spent most of his life being mistaken for a basketball player when really, he was a musical prodigy, a violinist. Quills seemed all rock-and-roll cool, but he was a sweetie pie.

"She's here, but so is some detective dude. Last night someone set your school on fire."

There must be many regular detective dudes in our city, but not many detective dudes who specialize in investigating suspected arson cases, because who do you think was standing in our living room, sipping a mug of chai tea, freshly brewed by Mrs. Dagnitz?

Yes. Robotective Huntington, he of the flat voice and glass Eye of Doom, wearing the same suit he was wearing the day I met him at Corbett Street Grocery. Was it the same suit? Or did he have a wardrobe of suits that were all the same?

He raised his robobrows just a smidge.

I could tell he was as surprised to see me as I was to see him.

Mrs. Dagnitz perched on the edge of the sofa, also sipping tea. My mother wore a pair of baby-blue linen pants, strappy gold sandals, and a long-sleeved aqua T-shirt. She looked like she was going somewhere, and then I remembered she *was* going somewhere. Shopping at the mall. With me. For shoes or undergarments or something. That was my second surprise of the morning—that she would imagine that after last night I would actually go anywhere with her, especially a place where there was a food court.

"Here's Minerva," said Mrs. Dagnitz. Ned, that traitor, had been sitting on her foot. When he saw me, he trotted over and sat down on my foot. I reached down and scratched the top of his head.

"Aren't you Angus Paine's friend?" said Robotective.

There was no point in saying I was or I wasn't, I could tell by the look on his face that he knew I was. "The one who's intrigued by fires?" he continued.

I remembered the day I'd met Detective Huntington, poking around the debris in the grocery with Angus. It was the day Angus had told me about Louise, and about how Detective Huntington was on the verge of declaring the fire an accident. "I'm not intrigued by fires," I said, trying hard to keep the tone out of my voice.

"Wasn't that you I saw sitting on the curb day before yesterday?"

I didn't say anything. This looked bad.

"I'm sure you heard there was a fire last night at Holy Family, where, I believe, you're going to be in eighth grade?" He looked at a small yellow pad of lined paper where he'd scribbled some notes.

"Quills just told me. What happened?"

"We're not going to go into that right now," said Robotective.

I knew from watching detective shows that he wasn't going to give any details in case I said something to trip myself up. It was an old detective trick. The detective says, "Sarah was murdered!" and the killer says, "Oh no! Who *stabbed* her?" And the detective says, "I didn't say *how* she was murdered! How did you know she was stabbed?"

"Is my school still *there*?" I asked, suddenly panic stricken. Where would I finish middle school? Would they make me go to public middle school? I'd wanted to go to public middle school since I'd found out the difference between private and public school. Now the thought of Holy Family burned to the ground made me dizzy.

"Yes, honey, yes, it's still there. It was just slightly damaged. It looks as if the fire started in the art room. By the time school starts in the fall, I'm sure it'll be—"

"Please, ma'am," said Detective Huntington.

"There's no need to frighten her," said Mrs. Dagnitz. I heard that familiar edge creep into her voice. You go, Mrs. Dagnitz. "Allowing her to think the worst."

"I'll tell you why I'm here, Minerva," said the detective. "Someone called in a tip saying you were at the school fairly late last night."

"Yes," I said. I tried to look as blank as possible. Kids who have gardeners for parents learn how to grow roses and kids who have artists for parents learn how to draw a box and kids who have lawyers for parents learn when to shut up, and when you're talking to law enforcement, that is exactly always.

This would have been my big chance to out my mother as the hot-food hurler that she was. I could have said, Yes! I had nowhere else to go! My mother drove me out of the house with her bad temper and bubbly mozzarella! But there was no way I was going to give him any more information than I had to. I twirled a piece of hair around my index finger, shifted my weight from one foot to the other, and waited.

He didn't say anything.

I didn't say anything.

I looked over his shoulder out the big living room window. It looked like the people across the street were getting a new front porch.

"Do you mind telling me what you were doing there?" asked Robotective.

"Sitting on the slide, talking to my boyfriend," I said. I was shocked to realize that I sort of meant Angus, instead of Kevin. Technically, I had talked to Kevin, though he hadn't talked to me.

"For how long?" he asked.

"A few hours."

"And you just sat on the slide? Did you see anyone around the building?"

"I saw a lot of people on the playground. Some boys playing basketball and a little girl with a dog." Suddenly, I remembered Daniel Vecchio and his loathsome posse of fifth graders riding their bikes down the street. "Was the person who called in the tip a kid? Because a lot of times with arson, the one who smelt it, dealt it."

"Yes, I think I've heard that before," said Robotective. Was he being sarcastic?

I told him about Daniel Vecchio, my fifth-grade nemesis, and how I had caught him stealing toilet paper out of the supply cabinet at school and reported him to Mrs. Grumble, the strictest teacher at Holy Family. I said that when Daniel Vecchio discovered it was me who'd ratted him out, he'd said he was going to get me. I told how only a few days earlier he'd egged our house and TPed it, too. "There's still paper in some of the branches," I said.

Detective Huntington had made a note of Daniel's name, then clicked the end of his pen and returned it to his shirt pocket. He hadn't written down a word I'd said.

"Why aren't you writing that down?" I asked.

He folded his hands in front of him and looked at me.

"She's not a suspect, is she?" asked Mrs. Dagnitz. Suddenly, I felt a rush of something other than pure loathing for my mother. She was not addicted to detective shows. She watched the cooking channel and *American Idol,* which made her a little slow.

"Let's just say she's a person of interest," said

Detective Huntington. "The caller didn't just place Minerva at the scene, they said they saw her start the fire."

Detective Huntington placed his mug on the mantel and said he would be in touch. He would most definitely be in touch, and we should most definitely not plan on going anywhere. As Mrs. Dagnitz walked him to the door, the heels of her little sandals slapping against the hardwood floor, she told him that actually soon we were headed to New York, where I would be part of an exciting world neurological conference. Certainly he'd read the nice profile of me in the paper? I was a special girl, a *very* special girl, a sensitive girl with special powers. Had he read the nice article about me in the paper? Did he know who Minerva Clark was? And, that, well, her father was an attorney?

I stood in the middle of the living room scratching my shin with the bottom of my foot, watching Mrs. Dagnitz say too much. Like always she started out okay—although bells went off in my head at her use of the word "we." Mark Clark was taking me to New York, not Mrs. Dagnitz—but then, she never knew when to hit the brakes. Did she really need to say I was special twice? Did she really need to remind Robotective that Charlie was a lawyer? Well, maybe that wasn't such a bad idea. It was never a bad idea just to remind people who wouldn't mind seeing your life ruined that you have an attorney in the family.

Robotective appeared to listen to her, but otherwise

said nothing. He looked over at me briefly before the door shut behind him and said, "I hope your tickets to New York are refundable, because I don't think you're going anywhere."

The minute the front door closed, Quills appeared. He'd been lurking in the computer room.

"What was that all about?" he said, cracking his knuckles, one after the other.

"Michael, don't do that," said Mrs. Dagnitz.

We stood in the entryway. Mrs. Dagnitz rubbed the crease between her eyebrows, looked over my shoulder, and frowned. "Is there a reason for that?"

I turned and saw her studying our lifesize cardboard James Bond in his tuxedo. I think it was the James Bond before the brand-new James Bond.

"Other than it's just one cool item?" asked Quills. For some reason he could get away with being borderline snotty and I couldn't. Unfair unfair unfair.

"There will never be a better James Bond than Sean Connery," sighed Mrs. Dagnitz. Then she pointed her blue gaze at me. "So, are you going to tell me about setting the school on fire?"

I felt like I needed a lawyer with *her*. "I don't know about setting the school on fire," I said carefully. "This is the first I've heard about it."

Mrs. Dagnitz sighed. "Is this because I've remarried? Is that what all this is about?"

"Huh?"

I glanced at Quills. He was cracking the fingers of his other hand and biting his lips. Quills could play the most smoking Led Zeppelin tunes of anyone I knew, but he was hopeless when it came to dealing with our mother. I wished Mark Clark was there, but he'd had to go back to work that day.

"I didn't set any fire, and nothing has anything to do with you being remarried," I said.

"Surely you don't think I believe you," said Mrs. Dagnitz. "I know you think I'm just some stupid middle-aged lady who doesn't have a clue, but I do know that you've turned into quite the little fib-teller."

"I am not a fib-teller," I said. Not exactly true. I was a fib-teller. Everyone was a fib-teller. Didn't Mrs. Dagnitz just tell Robotective that I was a sensitive girl? I wasn't a sensitive girl with special powers. It was a little fib told so that Robotective might go easy on me. Realizing this, I tried to stop-and-be-calm, like we were taught to do in the conflict management section of health class last year. I took a deep breath. "I'm telling you the truth."

"Is this like the truth you told just the other day? When you said you'd been at your friend Chelsea's house, when really you were doing God knows what with Kevin?" said Mrs. Dagnitz. She'd sidled up closer to me.

I twirled a lock of hair. When had I lied about being with Chelsea when I'd really been with Kevin? *Think, Minerva, think.* The only time I'd ever hung out with Kevin anywhere else but here at Casa Clark was when he'd just returned from fly-fishing in Montana and his mother invited me over to dinner. She'd made barbecued chicken and coleslaw with purple cabbage, then Mark Clark had picked me up and we'd stopped on the way home for Baskin-Robbins ice cream.

"I never lied about that," I said.

"Minerva, please. Stop now while you're ahead."

"I'm not lying," I said.

"The day we were late for the appointment with Dr. Lozano? And you came speeding up on that . . . whatever that thing was, that scooter? I held my tongue. I didn't even want to know where you got that thing. Are you a thief, too?"

"That day," I said. "I wasn't with Kevin. I was with Angus Paine." The words were on their way out of my mouth and I knew I'd made a monster mistake. It was like the time I helped my friend Hannah clean her goldfish bowl. I kept watch over Romeo and Juliet, swimming around in the bathroom sink, their temporary home, while Hannah scrubbed out the bowl in the kitchen. After she was finished, and had replaced the rocks and the pink plastic seaweed, and Romeo and Juliet were ready to be returned to their bowl, she'd called out "Done!" and for reasons I will never understand, I hit the stopper and the plug opened.

The instant Angus's name left my lips, I felt that same sick way I had watching poor Romeo and Juliet swirl down the drain to their deaths.

"Angus Paine, Angus Paine. Would that be the same Angus Paine you promised me you'd have nothing to do with?"

"I didn't promise, I said 'fine,' and I never said I was with Kevin that day. *You* said I was with Kevin," I said.

"Do not, *do not* insult me by splitting hairs about your lies, Minerva Clark." She wagged her finger in my face. Then she fluffed her bangs and cleared her throat. She was now leaving the planet of the purely POed and winging her way to the land of the long-suffering. I could tell. I'd been reading her signs for almost fourteen years. "All right," she said. "I suppose we should get your father on the phone. You're going to need good representation."

"Mom, I'm not going to need representation. I didn't do anything."

"And you're also going to need something decent to wear in court. I know you resisted getting your hair straightened, but to a jury you'll look more trustworthy if you have nice smooth hair. I've read studies."

"Oh, for God's sakes, Mom!" Quills blurted out. "Are you on crack? Min's not going to court, and she's not straightening her hair. Morgan was walking the dog last night and saw her sitting on the slide talking on her cell, just like she said."

"Don't you start, too," she said, turning on her heel. She collected her giant purse from the end of the sofa and started toward the door. "You know the testimony of a family member doesn't mean a thing."

I felt like I was under house arrest, like I already had one of those electronic cuffs around my ankle. Quills poured us each a bowl of Cap'n Crunch. He'd hidden the box in his room so Mrs. Dagnitz wouldn't see it. Quills asked about Angus Paine, and over two bowls of illegal cereal I told him the whole saga. I didn't like being called a liar—even though technically Mrs. Dagnitz was right, I had told her I was at Chelsea's house when I wasn't—and so I made sure I told the exact truth about this mystery as I knew it.

I told Quills how Angus Paine had read the story about me in the paper and called to see if I could find out who'd set the fire at his family grocery store. I told him how strange Angus was, how he could be both cold and distracted, then almost too warm and friendly, how he forgot to mention things that most people would find important but that he did not. I told him about my two suspects who didn't pan out—wheelchair-using Paisley O'Toole, who was too nice for her own good, and the verging-on-hysterical Wade Leeds, who lived in his car.

Then I summoned up my courage and told him about how I believed that Louise, the unhappy household ghost who lived in the walk-in freezer, was responsible for the fire. I said it was not uncommon for ghosts, especially Kikimoras, to go ballistic when their immediate environment was upset, and how Nat and Nat, Angus's parents, had been redoing a section of their grocery to make room for Paisley's new dessert counter.

"I know it probably sounds woo-woo stupid, but Quills, I saw Louise freaking out with my own eyes. I was at the grocery and Angus's mom has this collection of antique toasters that escaped the fire. Suddenly the levers of the toasters all started going up and down. All of them at the same time. And then the freezer door—the door to Louise's house, I guess you'd say—swung open . . ."

Quills drank the leftover milk in his cereal bowl, licked his lips, and said, "I'm not saying I don't believe in ghosts. It's like how I'm not totally convinced all of human life isn't just one long test-tube experiment being performed by God. I mean, who knows, right? But that said, you do know that it's a piece of cake for someone to do what you're talking about."

"What do you mean?"

"I mean, like, remember when Mark Clark was deep into his haunted house phase? Nah, you must have been too little. He'd figured out a way to make a rocking chair rock, and he also stuck eyes in a skull and could make those click back and forth. It's some animatronic thing. You should ask him."

"So, what are you saying, maybe the whole thing was staged?"

"Just tossing it out there as a possibility."

I cleared the table and loaded the dishwasher, being

extra careful not to allow one plate, bowl, or drinking glass to touch anything other than the plastic prongs that held them in place on the washer racks. It took forever, but I didn't mind. I knew when it was time to chillax, and this was one of those times. I would not leave the house, for fear that somehow I would be accused of returning to the scene of the crime, as arsonists were known to do. I would play with Jupiter and work on my rebuses and IM Reggie. I would think about Quills's just-tossed-out-there possibility. I would ponder it. I would take the possibility to the next level, which is that someone had rigged up those toasters on purpose.

I'd been squeezing out the sponge. I stopped in mid-squeeze. I was a pure one hundred percent idiot. Why hadn't I done this before? I tossed the sponge in the sink and dashed to the computer room, where I Googled "Angus Paine."

What I found made all the horrible sense in the world.

– 11 –

Of the thirty-seven hits for Angus Paine, there were six for an Australian high-jumping champion named Angus Paine and an Angus Paine who sold fancy motor homes. Also roaming the test-tube experiment known as Earth is an Angus Paine who grows daffodils beloved by the queen of Sweden.

My Angus Paine, it turns out, was a boy who lived—small world!—in Portland, Oregon, a kid just a bit older than me, whose full name was Caleb Angus Paine-Presinger, who used to go by Caleb Presinger until he suffered an electric shock while trying to build an electric chair for his haunted house and became the laughing-stock of the nation for about a week and a half.

There were a few news stories about my Angus Paine, and his name change was mentioned by someone who kept a blog devoted to the art and science of creating a truly scary haunted house. The blogger told how there had been a small story in the local paper (*The Oregonian!* The same paper that had profiled me!), and then the national news services had got ahold of it and made Caleb Presinger sound like some zany preteen mad scientist. A few late-night comedians had made some jokes about this dumb kid who'd received the shock of his life, and people had e-mailed them back and forth like mad for a few days. Caleb Angus Paine-Presinger became known as the Geek Idiot Who Tried to Build His Own Electric Chair, and that's when he decided to change his name.

I slumped back in the chair and pressed my fingers against my eyes. For a few seconds I watched the colors swirling behind my lids. Once I'd heard Weird Rolando say he couldn't get his head around something and I'd had no idea what he was talking about. Some of those old-time hippie expressions are baffling. What does it really mean to get your groove on? Does anyone really know? But now I got it. My head could get around Angus Paine the Hedger and Angus Paine the Moody Freak Flirt Monster and maybe even Angus Paine the Cruel Prankster, who'd rigged up his mother's antique toaster collection to scare me, but I could not get my head around the fact that Angus Paine was the one other person besides me in the known world who'd suffered an electric shock and then a personality change.

I thought back to my first appointment with Dr. Lozano. She had worn a maroon handwoven vest with crocodiles on it, and I remembered thinking how un-doctor-like that was. I was there because there was *some concern* that my brain had been messed up in some way after my accident. Dr. Lozano had made me draw a self-portrait and take a bunch of tests that measured my self-esteem. I tried to picture her with her gold nose ring and spiky dark hair, sitting behind her desk making a tent with her fingers, telling Mark Clark that she'd seen only one other case like mine, and it was that of a kid named Caleb Presinger, a.k.a. Angus Paine.

So, what did this mean? That Caleb/Angus had also received a giant dose of self-esteem, and now thought he was perfect just the way he was? I thought about the times we'd hung out. He'd thought he was pretty funny, but every boy I knew thought he was a laff-riot, whether he was or not. The last time I'd talked to Angus on the phone he'd seemed too worried about having insulted me, or whatever. Wasn't being obsessed about how you came off to other people a sign of insecurity?

I sat up and stared at the computer screen without seeing anything. I just didn't know. How could I know? I was no expert. But I knew someone who was.

Dr. Lozano never answered her phone. She had a special answering service where you could leave your messages that were screened by a live human being. The two other times I'd called her—once when I'd wanted to ask her whether she thought my new self-esteem could wear off, like a magic spell or a temporary tattoo, and once to ask her the exact days we'd be in New York City for the medical conference and whether she thought there'd be time to go to see *Wicked*, which Chelsea de Guzman said totally rocked—and both times she'd called me back in a few days. I didn't have a few days, but it was worth a try. I looked up her office number online.

"Hi, Dr. Lozano, it's me, Minerva Clark. I'm calling about that boy you told me about named Caleb Presinger, a.k.a. Angus Paine. It turns out I know him. I have a question about what happened to him after he got electrocuted. Oh! And I am sooo excited about our trip to NYC. It's going to rock, and of course be supereducational, too. Call me."

I'd just pressed the End button on my phone and slid it into my back pocket when my wild gorilla ring tone sounded. *Oooo-oooo-oooo-ahhnn!* It was Dr. Lozano, calling me back.

"Hi, Minerva, I got your message."

"I just had a question about that boy you told me about, Caleb Presinger, who changed his name to Angus Paine."

She hesitated. "What was your question?"

"What happened to him? Was it like with me? Did he score like I did on all those tests? Did his self-consciousness and all that disappear, too?"

"That's more than one question." She laughed, a bit uneasily, I thought.

I didn't say anything else. The computer room was on the side of the house that faced the street my school was on. I looked out the window and tried to see over the pink rhododendrons and down the block. I knew I wouldn't be able to see the school, but if the fire had been huge enough, maybe they'd blocked off the street. I couldn't see a thing but a tangle of leathery rhody leaves, and over that, two neighbors standing on the sidewalk talking.

"How do you know Angus?" asked Dr. Lozano.

I couldn't bear to spell it all out. "He tracked me down after that story ran in the newspaper. Did you see it? The one—"

"Tracked you *down*?" She sounded worried or something. I couldn't tell. This entire conversation was putting me into a moody freak mood.

"He called to say 'hey,'" I amended.

"Then you know he's a patient of mine, just as you are," said Dr. Lozano.

"Well, he didn't exactly say that. He never mentioned it at all, actually. I found out on the Internet."

She sighed. "It's an amazing invention, isn't it. The Internet."

"It is," I said. Duh.

"Minerva, look. I can't tell you anything about Angus. It's called patient-doctor privilege."

"I know. Lawyers have the same thing."

"What I can tell you is that Angus did experience a change after his accident, but it wasn't the same one as you did. Or rather it was, but it manifested itself in a different way. I hope that makes sense, because it's all I can really say."

Manifested? I knew what a manifesto was. Mark Clark's nerdy friend from work, DeMaio, had one—it involved changing how people paid taxes; I never listened—but I was a little unsure about "manifested."

"All right," I said.

"And Minerva," she said suddenly, as if she'd just thought of something, "you're not involved with Angus, are you?"

"Involved? Like, is he my boyfriend?"

"Yes, that's exactly what I meant."

"No," I said. When I heard myself say this, I felt sad and mad in equal measure. Sad because I'd grown to wish Angus was my boyfriend, and mad because from the beginning he'd been jacking me around. How much he'd been messing with me was the bigger question.

Dr. Lozano and I talked a little about New York—the trip was only two weeks away, a short time in Adultland but a long time in Kidland—and how we should definitely try to see a Broadway musical and buy a hot dog from a street vendor on Fifth Avenue. I didn't tell Dr. Lozano that if Robotective Huntington was going to pin the fire at Holy Family on me, I wouldn't be going to New York, or anywhere other than juvy.

For the rest of the afternoon, I did something I haven't done since I got into the mystery-solving business—made Mark Clark's Famous Kettle Corn and watched six straight hours of Animal Planet. I did a report on kettle corn in fifth grade. It was America's first snack food, made by the New England colonists in big iron kettles. It is exactly as sweet as it is salty, and delicious in its zit-creating goodness.

As I shoveled in the kettle corn, and watched the parade of lemurs, Cuban crocs, tiger sharks, and three-legged dogs that could do simple math, I called Mark Clark at work and asked him to explain how you might go about animating a bunch of toasters.

"You and Reg up to something?" he asked.

I was not about to lie. As Mrs. Dagnitz said, it was pernicious. I didn't know what that meant, but I'm sure it had to do with lying getting you in more trouble than just telling the truth, however sticky, icky, or inconvenient it was.

"No, I think I'm being punked by someone," I said.

"Oh, okay," he said. "What do you need to know?"

Apparently, truth is like Tabasco sauce—all you needed was a little. Mark Clark didn't ask who was trying to punk me, or what they were trying to do, or anything. He probably just wrote it off as some boring teenage saga.

Instead, he launched into a Mark Clark lecture about servos, short for servomechanisms or servomotors. They're called servos because they serve to turn a smaller mechanical action into a larger mechanical action. Radio-controlled cars depend on servos for all their action. Disneyland as we know it would not exist without servos. The Jungle Ride hippos that rise up and threaten each boatload of passengers at the exact same place in the river? Servo-driven. The hundreds of kicking, spinning, hopping, singing dolls of It's a Small World? It's a servo after all! Those silly pirates of the Caribbean chasing wenches while looting and pillaging? Yo ho, yo ho, a servo's life for them.

By the time Mark Clark got to how servos were used in the Haunted Mansion with its fake, chain-rattling ghosts, I could have rigged up those toaster levers myself.

I felt stupid, suddenly. I switched off a show about a frog infestation in Hawaii and closed my eyes. The kettle corn had given me a stomachache. Of course there was no ghostly arsonist lurking in the walk-in freezer at Corbett Street Grocery. There was, however, Angus Paine, who was up to something, and I had no clue what.

I summoned up every strange thing he'd ever done or said, everything I'd written off as being just how boys were, or just how this boy was. The way he was so different in person than on the phone. The mood swings.

The lies and half lies he'd told about the store being burned to the ground when it wasn't, about Grams Lucille being Wade's grandmother and not his mother, about not remembering Paisley, about how he said we'd meet at his house and not at the grocery—I *knew* he'd said the grocery! Why had he lied? And of course, his failure to tell me he was the boy version of me, the young teen who'd suffered a terrible electric shock and lived to create trouble.

I had no alternative but to wait until it was dark. I had to be sure Detective Huntington was off the clock, and not wandering around the grocery to see if I'd show up. It didn't take much to figure out that if Robotective was determined to blame me for the Holy Family fire, he might also tag me for the Corbett Street Grocery fire. He could arrest me for every unsolved arson in the city, for all I knew. There would be a new profile in the paper—Minerva Clark, girl detective–turned–serial arsonist.

Mrs. Dagnitz and Rolando were meeting some old friends for Indonesian food and a gamelan concert, so Mark Clark was free to bring home burritos, greasy chips, and chunky guacamole from our favorite divey Mexican place. Quills was at work, and Morgan was in class. We put their foil-wrapped burritos in the fridge, for them to heat up when they got home. We opened the dining room windows and put on a CD of Weird

Al Yankovic alternative polkas. Mark Clark and I were the only ones who could stand Weird Al, so we always waited until it was just the two of us to listen.

During dinner our dad, Charlie, called from Cincinnati and asked about Detective Huntington's visit. Unlike Mrs. Dagnitz, whose default setting was hysteria, Charlie was always as calm as a baby nurse. He did not appear to think I needed representation and immediate hair-straightening for a pending court appearance. He said he knew I didn't do it, without even having to ask.

I could tell Mark Clark would spend the entire night playing Everquest, because before he disappeared into the computer room he did some Speed Parenting. "You should get to bed early tonight since tomorrow is Mom's reception and you'll be staying up late. Did you take your vitamins today? Did you feed the dog? Does Jupiter have water? Try not to worry too much about what's going on, it'll all work out. Good night!"

When I left around ten o'clock, with Jupiter tucked in my backpack, I walked right out the front door.

I usually wasn't allowed to ride my bike after dark, and by the time I got to the grocery, I believed this was a ridiculous rule, especially in the summer. All across our city people were hanging out on their porches, sitting in cafés and at bus stops, throwing backyard parties that spilled out onto front lawns, and of course, pedaling around on their bikes.

Southwest Corbett Street was so lively—front doors thrown open to catch some cool air, a couple of kids playing Frisbee beneath the streetlight, a block party—I thought I should have waited until midnight, but the end of the street where the darkened grocery huddled beneath a flickering streetlight was quiet.

As I tugged on the padlock, I thought about the different kinds of anxious I'd been in this place. The first time I was jittery seeing up close the weird sort of damage only a fire could do. The second time I was startled and shaken by my run-in with Wade Leeds. The third time I was plain old scared to death by the antics of a "ghost."

I pulled a flashlight from my backpack. This time, I wasn't afraid to be here, or afraid of what I might find. I was afraid of how I would feel once I found it.

I crunched through the debris in my red-and-blue Chucks, the ones with the skulls on the ankles, shined my light on the singed Lucky Charms box, the half-burned potato chip bags, a snarl of metal chairs in one corner, and the empty deli case. When I reached the metal shelf with its row of retro toasters, I put down my backpack and fetched Jupiter.

I petted him a bit, just to make sure he was awake and alert. I needed him to be extra nosy and interested in anything small and shiny he could spirit away. Ferrets aren't afraid of heights. I set Jupiter on the end of the shelf, hoping he would nose around the toasters and not leap to the floor and disappear into the charred rubble.

He trotted to the first toaster and tried to stick his head inside one of the bread slots, but it was too narrow. He sniffed around the bottom, circled it twice, then moved on to the second one. I followed his movements with the yellowish beam of my flashlight. The toasters gleamed and Jupiter's fur looked clean and white. The rest of the store was dark, except where the streetlight shone in a window. It was sort of glam, as if it were a performance, spotlight on Jupiter.

The second toaster, like the first, had bread slots. These were wide enough for Jupiter to crawl into. He disappeared for a moment, then popped back out. He skipped the third toaster and went straight to the fourth toaster, one of the smaller, triangular-shaped ones with little feet, and side doors that pressed the bread against the toasting coils.

The doors were both open. Jupiter peeked in, grabbed on to something that struck his fancy, yanked it out, and immediately began dragging it off, searching for a place to hide his treasure.

I had to stand on my tiptoes to grab him off the shelf. It occurred to me that I could have gone upstairs to Grams Lucille's old apartment and borrowed the red ladder, if it was still there. But this was better. Just like the ferrets employed by telecommunications experts to pull the cables through the narrow tunnels beneath the cathedral where Prince Charles married Lady Diana, making it so the whole world could watch the wedding on TV, Jupiter enjoyed a job well done. I took the object he found from between his teeth, petted his head, and returned him to the backpack.

I studied the servo for a second. It was a square silver box with some wires on one end and a propeller-looking thing on the other. I exhaled loudly. Now what?

"Now that's what I call a sigh," a voice said from behind me.

It was Angus Paine.

– 12 –

"Oh look! It's Caleb Presinger!" I shined the flashlight straight into his chocolate M&M's–colored eyes. I held my arm against my side to steady my hand. I was not about to let him see me shake.

"Took you long enough to figure that out." He broke out his lopsided grin as if this situation were nothing but normal. "Don't you, like, Google everyone, first chance you get?"

"So you want to tell me about this?" I held up the servo, then pushed it into my side pocket. I didn't want him to rush me and grab it out of my hand.

"Can't see what you're holding with the light in my eyes." He shielded his eyes with his hand and took a step forward. The rubble crunched beneath his step.

"You don't need to see it. It's Louise. Or the servo

you used to make me think it was Louise. Actually one of the servos. I'm sure all the toasters have one."

"I feel bad about that. You looked really scared when you ran out of here. I didn't mean to scare you."

So I hadn't left him sitting at home watching the Discovery Channel in his narrow raspberry-colored house after all. I thought back to his kiss, the way I'd swung down his shady block, picked the daisy and tried to tuck it behind my ear. He'd followed me. He'd followed me here, then hidden somewhere, watching my reaction to his nasty little trick.

"Are you stalking me?" I blurted out.

"No, I wouldn't say that." He stuck his hands in his pockets, kicked at something with the toe of his back low-tops. Still smiling. Caleb/Angus wasn't humiliated at all. He didn't act wrongly accused, or have a raft of excuses for what he'd done. Maybe this was how his self-esteem showed up. He felt free to do anything he pleased, no matter how it affected anyone else.

"Then what is going on, Angus, or whoever you are? You never wanted me to solve the mystery of who torched this place, did you?"

"I did, sort of. I still think it was arson. But the truth is, I just wanted to hang out with you."

"You didn't think of just calling up and saying, 'Hey, I'm the other kid that got electrocuted, I'd love to hang out'?"

"We weren't electrocuted, Min," he laughed. "That means—"

"I know, I know, electric shock, whatever." I let my guard down half an inch. Maybe he wasn't going to attack me after all.

"You mean, if I would have just called and said, 'Hey, Minerva Clark, let's hang out,' you would have said yes?"

"Yes. I don't know."

"Oh come on. Be honest," he said. "You never would have had anything to do with me if I hadn't had a mystery to dangle in front of your nose. Look at me. And look at you."

I considered this. Was I really out of his league?

"Could you turn the flashlight off?" he asked.

"No, but we can go outside." I shouldered my backpack and stomped past him, making myself as tall and straight as the tallest tree in our yard. I noticed he waited until I was out of the building until he followed. He turned and snapped the padlock shut.

"So is that lock even broken?"

"Nah," he said. "I just left it half open so you could get in."

He sat on the curb beneath the flickering streetlight. His hair was brown in the sad light, not the copper-penny color I knew it to be. Across the street I could hear the late-night news blaring through an open window, and the scent of some night-blooming flower filled the air. "Sit next to me," he said, patting the narrow concrete strip beside him.

"Are you totally insane?" I said, a little louder than I meant to.

"Well, I do have some problems, yes. One of them is having fallen so hard for you, Minerva Clark, goddess of all that stuff I quoted to you the other day. It was dumb of me to set up the toaster thing, really dumb. But you were going through suspects so fast, I had to do something to keep you around. I really thought I'd have you going on Wade Leeds for a while. Talk about totally insane."

I recalled racing here on Angus's Go-Ped after my chat with Paisley O'Toole at her pastry shop. I'd sat on the curb eating my snickerdoodle, cussing Angus out in my head for being late. "So you never planned on meeting me here. You told me to come here so I'd run into Wade."

He nodded like a waiter who's just been told the meal tastes good. "He'd called my mom the night before and told her he wanted to get some stuff out of Grams's attic. I thought it'd be interesting to see you two connect."

"But how did you know to call me the minute he drove away?"

"I saw you."

He *was* a stalker. He'd watched me walk Wade Leeds to his dusty Explorer filled with all his junk, then he'd scampered home so he could be there when I arrived, acting as if he'd been waiting for me. I said nothing.

"And tracking down Paisley!" he crowed. "You really should work for the FBI or somewhere. That blew my mind. Paise is like a total angel. She used to babysit me before she was paralyzed."

Caleb/Angus wasn't looking at me, which would have required him to turn around. He was talking into the empty night, hanging out with the curb and the parking strip. I stood behind him on the sidewalk, holding my bike, ready to speed off if I had to.

"Let me just ask you one thing," I said.

"Will you sit next to me then?"

"Sure," I said.

"What do you wanna know?"

"Did you set the fires?"

"Fires, plural?"

"The one here, and the one at my school?"

He twisted around and looked at me. In the dim light I could see that chipped tooth. "Nope. I may like creating my little schemes, but I'm not into fire."

"And your mom's hip replacement?"

"I told you *that*?" He chuckled and shook his head—amazed at what? His own ability to make up the most random whoppers? "Nat's a marathon runner. Her hips are fine."

I turned my bike around and pedaled off without saying a word. My stomach felt like a wrung-out washcloth, my lungs like an air mattress that's had all the air pressed out of it. Dots danced before my eyes. It's amazing how fast you can ride a bike feeling like you're going to faint.

As I turned the corner onto my street and saw Casa Clark, the silly Mexican restaurant house among all the pretty bungalows and Portland colonials, dark except for the light on the third floor—my bedroom light—and the blue light of the screen in the computer room, I felt what the nuns at Holy Family were always on us about: gratitude.

Inside, I don't think Mark Clark had moved an inch while I'd sneaked out of the house aged thirteen and sneaked back in aged thirty-five, or whatever age you are when you realize people can surprise you in ways that will bring you to your knees.

I returned Jupiter to Ferret Tower and made a beeline upstairs, taking the steps two at a time, hitting speed dial for Reggie as I went. He answered before the end of the first ring, then dropped the phone. There were shuffling, scuffling sounds, and Reggie muttering before I heard "Yo!"

"Did I wake you up?" I asked.

"Nada chada baby," he said. "Whas'up?"

"Liar. You've been asleep since eight thirty."

"Nine thirty, but don't put that on your MySpace page. I don't want word to get out that I'm a pathetic loser with no social life."

I lay on my bed and stuck my bare feet up on the wall,

like Mark Clark had asked me a million times not to do. I told him the entire saga of Caleb Presinger/Angus Paine, beginning with the phone call. I knew Reg had heard this part before, but it felt important to start at the beginning. Reg was my best friend, and you know how I know? He let me tell the part he'd already heard. I finished up with the lie Angus had told about his mother's hip replacement. For some reason that lie was the freakiest one of all because there was absolutely no reason for it, other than the pure joy of telling it.

"Man, that is one messed-up dude," said Reggie.

"Hey, thanks, I think I got that."

"You do know he's your ghost, right? He set the grocery on fire, and probably the school, too."

"He's probably trying to frame me then for some reason?" I cleared my throat. My voice was so quiet I thought perhaps I hadn't said this aloud, but had only thought it. I recalled again sitting on the curb in the blazing sun, eating my snickerdoodle, waiting for Angus, who was never going to show up, when Robotective cruised by in his dark blue Dadmobile.

"Sure looks like it," said Reggie. "Didn't you say that detective said someone had called and told him you'd set the fire? Who else would do that?"

"Daniel Vecchio and his posse of loathsome fifth graders?"

"Dude, I don't even think that kid knows how to dial a phone, forget using one to call the fire marshal."

"But why would Angus want to frame me?" I asked. "That's the bigger question."

"Other than that he's a total head case? We say people are whacked, or crazy, or whatever, but this guy sounds truly mental. It's called being a sociopath. And no one knows why sociopaths do what they do. It's part of why dudes like him are so fiercely dangerous. He could have just set both fires because he finds it entertaining, the same way you like to solve mysteries."

All of a sudden, it felt late. I was thirsty and tired. I put my pillow over my eyes. "So, if it *was* Angus—"

"Minerva! It was Angus! He's an evil creepmeister, all right? Every bad or suspicious thing that's gone down since you got that phone call goes straight back to him, okay? Quit giving him the benefit of the doubt."

"I was just thinking out loud," I said weakly.

"Oh, that is so much horse pucky. You girls always like the bad boys. It makes us nerds feel even worse than we already do."

"But he looked me right in the eyes when I asked him if he started the fires and he said no, he was into creating little schemes, but he wasn't into fire." I wasn't about to mention that he'd also called me a goddess, which was probably the first and last time in my life that was ever going to happen.

"But that right there was the creation of another little scheme, don't you see? You found that servo, evidence of his pure nut-job evilness, and you still hung out and had a conversation. You still thought he was worthwhile enough to ask him whether he'd set the fires. You should have known by then that every syllable that comes out of his mouth is a lie."

"All right! I got it! Point taken!" I said. I threw the pillow across the room and sat up. "Then if I'm being framed, I need to find out why he's doing it, so I can figure out what he's going to do next." I had no faith that I could actually do this, but it sounded good, and all of us Clarks are firm believers in faking it until you make it.

"That's the spirit, old girl!" Reg said in his fake British accent.

"But how?"

"Didn't you say that lady at the pastry shop is an old friend of the family? Nothing he said is worth diddly, but if the info came from her, maybe she knows something."

This cheered me up. Maybe I could solve this mystery after all. "Reg, that's a good idea."

"That's why I get paid the no bucks," he said. "Now can I go back to sleep?"

In the morning I came downstairs and Morgan was sitting at the dining room table eating a piece of cinnamon toast and reading a paperback book with very tiny writing.

"Where is everybody?"

He looked up from his book. He wasn't wearing his

earflap cap, which meant it was going to be another scorcher. "Getting ready for tonight, I guess."

"Well," I said, "I need to go do something." I plucked his piece of toast from the plate and tore off a bite. "I'll be back in a little while."

"I'd hang around if I were you," he said. "In case Mom shows up." His eyes drifted back to his book. I could tell he couldn't care less. His mind was chasing some brainiac idea, and that was more important than whether I was going out on a Saturday morning for a few hours.

Because Paisley's on 23rd was a pastry shop, it opened early, along with all the Starbucks and coffee places that were Not Starbucks. The rest of the shops on Northwest Twenty-third were still closed. Not many people were on the sidewalks, which had been hosed down earlier in the morning by invisible city workers.

I crossed my fingers that since it was Saturday, Paisley would be there. It had to have been one of her busiest days of the week, right? Or if not, at least there were no doctors in their offices, so she couldn't have yet *another* doctor's appointment.

The bell over the door jingled as I walked in. Yet another girl was at the counter—this one with a crew cut—but I spied Paisley in the back, giving instructions to the elf-like baker.

"Excuse me!" I called out. Desperation had made me bold. Before I'd drifted off to sleep, the pieces had started falling into place. I realized that unless I nailed Angus for both fires, I would always be a suspect, waiting for Robotective to show up at the door with the handcuffs.

Paisley drove herself right over and asked what she could do for me. She didn't say, "Can I help you?" which often sounds like "What do you want from me now?" She asked how could she help me. How *could* she help me?

Save my life, I wanted to say. Keep me out of juvenile hall. I noticed again Paisley's square white teeth. She was so clean and pretty. I felt like throwing myself at her feet like a zealot in a trance and begging her to help me, help me!

I sat at the small metal table near the front window. "You don't look very good," Paisley said. "Should I call someone for you?" She reached a curled hand out and laid it on my knee, then turned to crew-cut girl. "Evie, could you bring some juice over?"

"I wanted to ask you a few things about Angus Paine," I said. And then like a big idiot, I started to cry.

"Oh dear," she said. "What's he done now?"

It turned out that since Angus suffered his electric shock two years ago, he'd been in nothing but trouble. He'd been kicked out of one school for stealing the frogs from the science room, and at another school he'd accused his pretty French teacher of hitting on him, a complete fabrication. Nat and Nat—they were such good people!—had taken him to doctors and tried different medications. That's why everyone was so excited when Dr. Lozano—another wonderful person—said she was going to take him to New York with her. He'd been so looking forward to it . . .

"What?" My tears stopped, sucked clean out of my head by the shock. "Dr. Lozano was taking Angus to New York? For the big brain-doctor conference next month? Is that what you mean?"

"She was giving a speech on—I don't know exactly—something to do with trauma to the young adolescent brain. Angus was going to be her example. Then there was the fire at Nat and Nat's grocery, and it was assumed Angus had something to do with it, and she just thought perhaps it would be better if she took someone else. Someone less troubled, I guess."

I drank some of the orange juice Evie had brought, just to have something to do. I remembered how, at my appointment with Dr. Lozano, she'd made that phone call to the conference organizers to make sure they had my name on the program. Didn't she say that she'd originally selected someone else? Oh man. I rubbed my forehead with my palm. "I guess I'm the less troubled one," I said.

"You?"

I gave her the condensed *TV Guide* version, how I, too, had suffered an electric shock that gave me loads of self-esteem that was uncommon in a kid my age.

"I don't know if his trauma gave him self-esteem, exactly," Paisley said. "It's more like it gave him license to do whatever he wanted to do, no matter the consequences. Or, that's the best they can come up with at the moment. At any rate, being uninvited to the conference sent him into a tailspin. He was not happy."

"When did Dr. L.—Dr. Lozano—uninvite him?"

"Two weeks ago maybe? Ten days? I'm terrible with time," she said, laughing.

Mere days before he'd called Minerva Clark, begging for her to help him solve a mystery.

"I want to be clear that they never arrested him for setting the store on fire. That was only conjecture on his parents' part. They're at their wits' end. No one found any evidence to suggest it was Angus, and I'd like to think it wasn't. He isn't a bad kid."

I tried to look into Paisley's eyes to see if she really believed that or was just trying to convince herself, but she was staring down at her small pink hands, crying a little herself.

– 13 –

I was *too* late.

As I pedaled up the street to Casa Clark, I saw Detective Huntington's dark blue sedan parked in front. Robotective was standing in our living room with his hands clasped behind his back, his face as blank as a dry-erase board on the first day of school. I noticed that this time no one had offered him tea.

It was a regular family reunion. Mrs. Dagnitz was sitting on the edge of the sofa in her sherbet-colored yoga outfit, sobbing into her hands. Weird Rolando sat beside her, rubbing her back. He wore braids on either side of his head and a purple T-shirt that said something woo-woo about the magic of yoga on it. Mark Clark was dressed in his usual polo shirt and khaki pants, standing at the living room window looking out at the neighbor's half-built porch. Morgan sat on the piano bench, scratching Ned behind the ear. Ned was panting with delight. Quills was probably still asleep, which was okay with me. There were enough people here to see me dragged off to jail for something I didn't do.

"Good morning, Minerva," said Robotective Huntington.

"What are you doing here?" I asked.

Mrs. Dagnitz looked up from her hands and opened her mouth. Dollars to doughnuts she was going to tell me not to be rude, but I shot her the stink eye, and her mouth fell closed. Didn't some famous person once say that the truth shall set you free? I didn't know about that, but one thing was for sure, it made you feel free to sass. After my freaky-weird encounter with Angus Paine at the grocery, where he admitted that he'd wired up his mom's toaster collection to make me think it was the Kikimora who set the fire, and Paisley O'Toole's juicy bit of evidence that Angus had been Dr. Lozano's original choice to go to New York for the brain-doctor conference, I was sure I had enough new information to keep myself out of juvy, at least for a few days.

Robotective Huntington stared at me for a long, awkward moment, and I stared right back at him. I could stand there all day. I was an eighth grader on summer vacation, after all. Just as I was trying to figure out how I would drop the gems from my own investigation into his hands, something happened that we in the Clark family call the First Cousin of a Miracle. Robotective Huntington had found a clue that would nail Angus Paine. The cool thing was, he didn't even know it.

"Can you tell me what this is?" he said slowly, as if I didn't speak English. He opened a small black-leather portfolio and pulled out a plastic bag marked EVIDENCE in orange marker. He dangled the plastic bag before me, but wouldn't let me hold it or touch it.

Inside was a scrap of paper the size of a piece of notebook paper. I cocked my head to read it. I recognized the bold red typeface, and the familiar picture of a sable ferret.

"It's from a bag of Only Ferrets ferret food," I said.

Robotective frowned. I tried to read the expression in his good eye. Nothing.

"This was found at the scene. Another piece of this was used to set the fire." He carefully placed the plastic bag back inside his case. Behind me, Mrs. Dagnitz made a noise that sounded like a cross between a tsk and a gasp.

"Yeah," I said. "And your point would be?"

"Minerva!" said Mrs. Dagnitz. I knew she couldn't help herself. I was a teenager sassing a grown-up. She was probably genetically programmed to butt in.

"I was told you have a ferret," Robotective said a little impatiently.

"I don't feed him *that* stuff, if that's what you're thinking. Never have. Never will."

"I'm afraid I don't follow." He was now exasperated. I felt a small prick of triumph. I was ruining his Saturday morning bust.

"She feeds Jupiter only cat food," said Morgan. "We just got a new bag the other day up at Green's Pet Food on Fremont. You can ask Mrs. Green."

"Cat food?" said Robotective.

"High-protein cat food is just as good as ferret food," I said. "Everyone who keeps ferrets knows that."

"You've never used Only Ferrets?"

"Never," I said. "It a total ripoff. Twice as expensive as cat food." I paused then, just for drama. "But I do know someone who has a torn bag of Only Ferrets sitting in his mudroom. And he doesn't even have a ferret."

A spark of intrigue showed itself in Detective Huntington's good eye. "Angus Paine has a bag of ferret food that matches this scrap?" he asked.

I smiled a big smile. A-ha! He'd fallen for the old detective trick. "I didn't say *who* had the bag, did I?"

Robotective Huntington rolled his thin lips inside his mouth and nodded. By robotective standards, it could probably have been considered a smile. I imagined that just like Cryptkeeper Ron and Wade Leeds, Robotective Huntington thought Angus Paine was bad news. And like Paisley O'Toole and Nat and Nat, he figured

Angus had had something to do with the grocery store fire, but he couldn't prove it. Detective Huntington was probably sick to death of Angus's lopsided smirk and phony good manners, the way he strutted around the grocery as if it belonged to him and not his parents. I am a detective and not a mind reader, but I would guess that he was the kind of man who would be dog-on-a-walk happy to nail Angus Paine to the wall.

"I need to check this out, of course," said Detective Huntington.

Mrs. Dagnitz hopped to her feet and started toward the door.

"I can let myself out," he said. "You're still a person of interest, Miss Clark. I'll need to investigate this a little further, but I still wouldn't leave town." Then he looked around the room at my brothers, and Rolando, who'd also leaped to his feet, and Mrs. Dagnitz, who was wringing her hands. "You've got quite a support crew here. I'll be in touch."

After the door clicked shut behind him, Mrs. Dagnitz wrapped her skinny arms around me and sobbed into my neck. This was the cue for all the men to bolt into the dining room. I heard the sound of puzzle pieces rattling around inside a cardboard box. Weird Rolando had brought over another eight-thousand-piece puzzle. I heard Morgan say, "Whatcha got there, Rollie?"

Rollie? Is it possible we'd get all blended after all?

Mrs. Dagnitz pulled herself together and blew her

nose into a wad of tissue. "The way you handled that! I could never have done that. You have no idea. Sometimes I'm just so proud of you."

"That is so not true," I said. "You're just glad I wasn't hauled off to the slammer on your wedding day." Yeah, I know, it wasn't her wedding day, and nobody but old-time gumshoes in black-and-white movies called it the slammer, but I didn't care.

"Of course I'm glad. I ordered you a special meal. If you were in prison, what would I do with it?" She smiled and gave my arm a squeeze. Here was another First Cousin of a Miracle—Mrs. Dagnitz joking around about her wedding reception being ruined.

"We never got my shoes," I said. She was being nice, so it was my duty to try to be nice back, wasn't it?

"Well, I know. We all just got so busy. I've been swamped. And of course, you've got your own life. You think I don't know that, but I do. I appreciate that this day means a lot more to me than it does to you. So, well, here, yesterday after hot yoga I swung by Nordstrom and picked up . . . well, here . . . go put your dress on and just try these on. I'm sure the perfect pair is in here somewhere."

She'd trotted into the entryway. Next to life-size cardboard James Bond were three large-handled bags, each one containing a stack of shoe boxes. She pulled out one stack after the next, opened the boxes, and lined up pair after pair of mostly dressy sandals, some light brown, some dark, with heels low and heels high. There was a bronze pair with a four-inch heel, and a pair of pink slides. "I didn't think you wanted the pink, but who knows? Maybe they'll work. Anyway, we can take back the ones you don't like. That's what we love about Nordstrom!"

"Mom, you're insane," I said.

And I wasn't lying.

For the rest of the day I did a whole lot of nothing. I tidied my room—the compromise I always make with Mark Clark when I don't want to clean it. Cleaning means dusting and vacuuming. Tidying means putting my dirty clothes in the laundry hamper and making my bed.

I should have just gone ahead and cleaned. Maybe it would have distracted me from thinking about what was going on over at Angus Paine's house. Maybe running the vacuum would have drowned out the sound of my imagined conversation between Robotective and Nat and Nat, where he told them that he now had hard evidence that their son was an arsonist. An arsonist and a murderer. I was pretty sure Angus hadn't meant to kill Grams Lucille, or anyone for that matter, and yet he had. It made what he'd done a million times worse. I remembered the wrecked look on the face of Wade Leeds, going through that green file cabinet, at all the things his mother had saved. Was he the one who'd found her that day, melted to the chair? I squinched my eyes shut as tight as I could, as if that would prevent me from thinking about it.

I sat on the end of my bed and played with a Beanie Baby—Finn the shark. I'd found him under my bed. For a minute I wished I was still a little kid who loved Beanie Babies and dreamed of the day I would publish my rebus notebook. What do parents do when they find out their kid is a monster? Then I had a thought that made my insides feel as if they wanted to escape straight through my skin: What would Angus do to me when he discovered that I was the one who'd turned him in? The last mystery I'd solved, the one about the missing rare red diamond, had ended when the thief had walked right into our house and threatened Mark Clark, Quills, and me with a gun.

I dropped Finn on the floor and bolted downstairs. Who was home? Who could I hang out with? Casa Clark was big enough that people came and went, and unless you were paying attention you'd never know. It was late afternoon, and the back door was wide open. A bee buzzed around the kitchen. I looked through the window over the sink and saw Morgan in the backyard trying to teach Ned to catch a Frisbee. I slammed that door and locked it. Morgan would just have to knock.

Mark Clark was at his post in front of his computer (in the very room where we were attacked by the jewel thief).

I scurried in, pulled up a chair, and asked if I could watch him play. Mark Clark knew I thought watching boys play video games was the most boring activity on planet Earth, more boring than cleaning my room.

"What's up with you?" He turned and looked at me. He had a crease between his dark eyebrows.

"What do you think that Angus kid will do when he realizes it was me who ratted him out? I mean, if he started a fire and everything . . ."

"Don't worry about it. They'll arrest him and at the very most release him into the custody of his parents. He's not going anywhere."

I must have looked doubtful, because he reached over and wiggled my knee. "Don't worry. It's fine. It's over."

"Why haven't we heard anything from the detective, then?"

"He's probably loaded with paperwork, or he just hasn't gotten to it yet. He's got other cases, don't forget. And anyway . . ." He checked the time on his computer. "It looks like it's time we started getting ready for the reception."

"Oh joy," I said. But the truth is, I was excited. I was looking forward to wearing my adorable brown halter dress and ordering a 7Up with a cherry in it.

The Wedding Reception of the Century was held at a historic building in an industrial area not far from Casa

Clark. It used to be a ballroom or a movie palace or something. Portland is loaded with old-time buildings that are redone by forward-thinking architects who spend millions of dollars renovating the building to its original splendor in an environmentally responsible way. I know all this because Morgan and Rolando yakked about it on the way to the party.

Kevin and I sat in the backseat with our pinkies touching, but not holding hands. He looked hot in his coat and tie, and he said I looked hot in my halter dress and strappy high-heeled sandals. I stared out the window as we drove, trying to imagine when we would see each other all dressed up like this again. Next year at my middle school graduation? Would we even still be boyfriend and girlfriend by then? It seemed like light-years away. Not that I know exactly how long a light-year is.

I must make a full confession. I had forgotten about Kevin. After the night I tried to tell him about being assaulted with the scalding slab of vegetarian lasagna, and he was too wrapped up in World of Warcraft and MiniVanDamme, I forgot about him. Or not forgot about him, exactly—set him aside. I knew from years of watching Mark Clark obsessively play his video games that I could catch up with Kevin again in a few days and he would be right where I'd left him, the big news being that MiniVanDamme was now level forty and had earned his epic weapon.

We arrived at the historic building just as the Purpley Time was settling in. People were milling around outside, tugging at their ties and gulping their drinks. Inside, the air-conditioning was broken, a motor burned out or something.

Poor Mrs. Dagnitz. Yes, I felt bad for her. Her blond hair was stuck to her head. The bridge of her nose was shiny with perspiration. She ran around making sure no one was dying of the heat. Since most of her friends were in tip-top shape, no one looked as if they were going to have a heart attack, but no one touched any of the beautiful food my mom had spent weeks agonizing over. There was supposed to be dancing, but the band played cringe-worthy soft-rock hits to an empty dance floor while everyone gathered at the bar ordering all those hot-weather drinks that are the adult cousins of the Slurpee. Things hadn't turned out the way she'd planned, and now she was trying to make the best of it. Rolando stood near the open door holding a drink, laughing with some other men. He didn't seem to mind at all.

Morgan stood listening, looking glummer than usual. Quills sat at a nearby table with a small plate of food in front of him. He was about the only person eating anything at the whole party. I pulled up a chair.

"Want an egg roll?" he asked.

"Don't chew with your mouth full," I said.

"Don't talk with your mouth open," he countered. Ha ha. Another old family joke.

I chewed on some ice from my drink. "What's wrong with Morgan?" I asked.

"He's got that girlfriend—would-be girlfriend, I should say. That chick who works at Roasted on Fremont. He asked her to come tonight and she said she had something else going on."

"Do you think she was lying?" I asked. Since knowing Angus Paine, it occurred to me that people probably lied a lot more than anyone ever imagined.

"Love is lies, baby sister." Suddenly, Quills shoved his plate away, grabbed a cocktail napkin, and pulled a felt-tip pen from his back pocket. "That's good. *Love is lies, baby sister.*" He then started jotting down some new lyrics for his band, Humongous Bag of Cashews. Here is a secret about Quills: He writes all his lyrics on tiny napkins. He thinks that when he becomes world famous, it will sound better in *Rolling Stone* magazine if it says he dashed off his lyrics on cocktail napkins instead of on a PC.

In her hostess frenzy, Mrs. Dagnitz decided Kevin was the most handsome teenage boy there. He was practically the only teenage boy there, but I was not about to argue. When she found out Kevin was a swimmer, she dragged him around to introduce him to some of her friends who were on a ladies' swim team. I bet they didn't swim the butterfly, the most show-offy stroke there is, or maybe they did. Middle-aged moms do all kinds of things these days to embarrass their teenage daughters, why not the butterfly? The good thing about Kevin is that he is polite. Oh, and he knows how to fold a lot of cool origami animals and boxes. And he's nice to me, except when he's playing video games. Is that good enough for a boyfriend? I don't know.

I was not about to follow them around listening to them compare times for the hundred-meter whatnot, so I took my 7Up and went outside, where it was a few degrees cooler. It was dark by now. Inside, the band was playing a song about sailing away. I sat on a low stone wall, set my drink beside me, and tied up my hair in a knot on top of my head. Much better. A trio of men talking about the best way to fertilize your lawn wandered back inside, leaving me alone.

It happened in an instant.

I heard the high buzz of a scooter, turned to look, and suddenly there was Angus Paine, leaping off his Go-Ped. It continued on, riderless, for a few yards, then crashed over. I didn't have time to say a word. He marched toward me, grabbed my arm, and hauled me backward over the wall. My glass of 7Up flew into the air, shattering when it hit the sidewalk. My hair fell out of its knot and one of my shoes came off.

Angus hauled me around the side of the building and into the bushes, where he clamped his hand around my throat.

"What in the hell was that stunt? Sending that

detective my way? You really upset my parents." His voice was high with hysteria. Had I never noticed that he looked like a hyena with his snappy pupil-less eyes and chipped tooth?

"Let go of me," I said. I grabbed his forearms, but couldn't pull them away from me.

"Answer my question, then I'll let you go," he said.

"Liar," I said. I knew this would only make it worse, but it made me mad. He just let any old thing roll out of his hyena mouth and called it the truth. I was sick of it.

"It's your own fault you're in this predicament, Minerva," he said.

"I could say the same thing to you. Maybe if you weren't an arsonist, Robotective wouldn't have been forced to hunt you down." I was surprised it was so easy to talk, since I was being strangled. We were between two huge bushes—the kind with small dark leaves and tiny white flowers that look like bells and bloom in the spring. He'd shoved me against the wall. I was afraid he was going to start banging my head against the stone if I didn't get out of there. But how? *Keep talking*, I thought, *keep talking. Keep him distracted.* "I'm really just curious why you did all this. Was it really just because you wanted to go to New York with Dr. Lozano?"

"I deserved to go. I'm extraordinary. Everyone says so. Even Dr. Lozano, before you started sucking up to her and took my spot."

"I think she picked me instead of you because you're a lunatic who does stuff like this," I said.

He tightened his grip around my throat. "Don't make it worse for yourself, Minerva. Why do chicks always do that? Make it worse for themselves."

"So are you going to kill me? If Dr. L. didn't want to take you to New York because you were an arsonist, she surely wouldn't want to take you if you were a murderer. But, wait, you are a murderer. Grams Lucille, remember her?"

"I will give you one more chance," he said, shaking me. "Call Huntington and confess to the Holy Family fire, and after New York I'll tell him it was me and they'll let you go."

"I'll get right on that," I said.

"I thought I knew you," he said. Was he starting to cry? "I thought you were cool."

"I am cool," I said. So cool, in fact, that I'd figured out how to get myself out of this. In the first mystery I'd ever solved, Tiffani, my old babysitter, used her shoe as a weapon. She wore those high-heeled wooden mules. My shoes didn't have that much heft, but if I could reach down, slip off the remaining one, and smash it over Angus's head, the surprise might cause him to let me go and I could make a run for it.

"This isn't over, you know. Nat and Nat have a good lawyer. They'll get me out of this, and then when you least expect it, you might smell some smoke in your own room, in that ugly house up there in that fancy neighborhood."

"You know where I live?" I heard the fear in my own voice. Dummy! I shouldn't have said a word.

Angus laughed. "I know everything, Minerva Clark."

"So you were stalking me."

"Research. It's called research. I'd hate to see your ferret fry, though. I really do want a ferret. Maybe I'll sneak in that basement window you have that doesn't lock and save him before I torch the place."

"You really are crazy," I said. "Thanks for saving Jupiter, though." Just as I leaned sideways to remove my shoe, I heard the sound of male voices.

"Hey! What's going on here?" It was Kevin, standing on the sidewalk. Rolando was right behind him.

"HELP!" I hollered. "He's strangling me."

Kevin tore Angus Paine off me with swim-champion strength. He dragged him out onto the sidewalk, threw him onto his stomach, and dug his knee into his back. Angus wasn't afraid, but irritated. "All right, all right," he said. "No need to get violent."

Rolando called the cops at 911. Kevin pulled off his tie with one hand and secured Angus's hands behind his back. I was too dazed to tell him how impressed I was. Where'd he learn how to do that?

I rubbed my throat. Now my knees shook, my legs trembled, my hands fluttered. Rolando fussed. He wanted to call the paramedics, too, but I wouldn't let him. The police showed up in three minutes flat, cuffed Angus, and stuck him in the backseat. Angus looked at us and sighed, "You're really overreacting here, folks."

As we watched the black and white drive away, I turned to Rolando to thank him and noticed that—guess what?—my stepdad had cut his hair.

- 14 -

That night, after the wedding reception, we sat around the picnic table in the backyard in our dress-up clothes, drinking pomegranate-juice iced tea—my mom's favorite—as I told my family the whole story. It felt weirdly like a holiday. Maybe it was the drama. Everyone was eager to put together the pieces. Rolando wondered whether Angus Paine had set the fire at the grocery just to have a mystery to solve, or he had some other reason.

"Another reason?" asked Mark Clark. "I'd say there's another reason—the kid's mental."

They got in a big discussion over the existence of ghosts, specifically Louise, the Kikimora. Someone went in the kitchen and retrieved a bag of pork rinds that must have been hidden somewhere.

Quills, who'd been on Cryptkeeper Ron's Tour of

Haunted Portland more than any of us, and considered himself an amateur expert, said he knew for a fact that Cryptkeeper Ron had his ghosts certified by a world-renowned professor of paranormal activity. Then they all talked about whether a professor of paranormal activity—whoever that might be—was a big crackpot anyway. Mark Clark said he thought it was all a ruse. Morgan said he didn't know whether he believed in that particular ghost, but he believed there were spirits at work in the world. I thought about my interaction with Louise, not the corny part with the animatronic toasters, engineered by Angus Paine, but the first day at the grocery when we opened the freezer door, and the air was still chilled even though the refrigeration unit had been off for days. Was that Louise? I still couldn't decide. Maybe it was like that in life—there were things about which you would never, could never, make up your mind.

Mrs. Dagnitz looked wrung out. She sat in a patio chair with Ned at her feet. She petted his soft fur with her toes. She didn't say anything. She kept pressing her fingers to her temples. I wondered whether she was freaking out about everything that had happened and wondering whether she should move back to Portland, where she could breathe down my neck every second of every day.

She called me over to her and grabbed my hand. "Honey, could you go inside—in my purse, there's a white bottle, it's my headache medicine. Could you bring it?"

The itty-bitty fancy purse she'd brought to the reception was on the kitchen counter. Nothing in there but a lipstick and her wallet. Slung around the back of one of the dining room chairs was her giant walking-around everyday purse, the one a small child could hide in with no problem. I stuck my hand in, felt around for a medicine bottle, and instead hit upon . . . an MP3 player?

My mother has an iPod?

I sat down at the dining room table and turned the pink metallic thing over and over in my hand. I couldn't help it. I had to have a listen. I expected some woo-woo yoga-y music, gamelan music, or bamboo flutes played by Incan mystics, or chanting monks or that Irish lady with the floaty voice. I thought the most extreme thing I would hear would be the Beatles.

Instead . . . well, I'm embarrassed to tell you some of the stuff my mom had on her iPod. Rap music. Heavy metal. A whole sound track from some skateboard movie. A really dirty song by a group Mark Clark will not even permit Quills to listen to in the house, in case I might accidentally hear some of the lyrics through his headphones.

As I listened to song after song, I realized I had never really known my mom. To me, she was this over-exercised, pastel-wearing control freak, but here she had Green Day—Green Day! My favorite band!—on her iPod. And not just the new stuff that everyone loved, but early punk Green Day that I thought no one knew about but me.

Wait until I told Reggie. I texted him there and then.

I must have sat listening for a long time. I felt a hand on my shoulder. It was my mother. "Did you find the medicine?"

"Green Day, Mom? You like Green Day?" I was not about to mention all the other stuff.

"Doesn't everyone?"

I wanted to say, *Everyone but people's mothers,* but I couldn't.

It just wasn't true.

Two weeks later Mark Clark and I took what's called the red eye to New York City. It's called the red eye because when you get off the plane, your eyes are red from exhaustion. But I was too excited to be exhausted. My dad, Charlie, performed some magic and upgraded our seats to business class, so we had bigger seats and better food. I even had my own personal television stuck in the back of the seat in front of me, and something called lumbar support. I still did not have an iPod—I sort of thought my mom might get me one after I'd discovered hers, but no dice—but there was so much else to do on the airplane that I didn't mind.

My mom and Rolando stayed in Portland a few extra days, to make sure I wasn't completely traumatized, then drove back to Santa Fe. They said they liked Portland and its green pines and gaudy rhododendrons, but the soppy heat was too much. It was much drier, and therefore more pleasant, in Santa Fe.

My mom didn't cook any more fish, nor did she force me to go shopping. She let me keep three pairs of the shoes she'd bought, and I went to yoga with her one day. My favorite pose is corpse pose, where you lie flat on your back and close your eyes. We never talked about her lasagna-throwing outburst, or how I sort of basically totally invaded her privacy when I listened to her iPod without asking. We have a truce going, for now.

Dr. Lozano, who did not want to fly on the red eye to New York, was going to meet us at our hotel. It had a minibar. I checked.

She also was able to get us tickets to see *Wicked* and said she knew where to buy the best cute fake purses, plus bootleg CDs and DVDs. I was supposed to pretend she didn't know anything about it, though, because if it got out, it might sully her good reputation. Reggie gave me twenty dollars to buy him a copy of the *Lord of the Rings* trilogy.

Dr. Lozano was shocked to hear about Angus's "behavior." That's a neutral doctor word for full-on psycho meltdown. Still, she wouldn't tell me anything more about his case.

Angus still would not admit his guilt, even though

Detective Huntington got a warrant and found a notebook beneath his mattress, where he talked about sneaking into the grocery at midnight. He'd hung on the ancient gas line until it broke, filling the store with the gas that exploded when the electric motor from the freezer kicked on. At Holy Family, he'd used part of the ferret food bag to set a trash can on fire, hoping it could be traced back to me.

Angus told the court that was all just something he'd made up, and the weird thing is, he may really believe it. Because Grams Lucille died in the fire at the grocery, they wanted to try Angus as an adult. He was almost fifteen. Detective Huntington said there was a good chance the court would put him away at least that many years.

It's about five hours from Portland to New York by plane. Mark Clark and I talked a lot about why Angus did what he did. Had he really set the first fire just to have a mystery to wave under my nose? Had he used the arson as a Minerva magnet, in the same way Morgan was using Ned as a Jeannette magnet? Or had he set the fire at the grocery purely for entertainment, as Reggie suggested, and then, after Dr. Lozano told him he couldn't come to New York, decided to find me and see if he could mess with my life enough so that I couldn't go either? Was it like, if I can't go, neither can that Minerva Clark? That was how Angus Paine's strange mind worked.

Before we left for the airport, I'd needed to do one

more thing before I closed the case. Angus lied about everything, but I had to double-check one last thing.

I fired up Mark Clark's computer and Googled "Minerva Clark." Eighteen hits were returned. There was the newspaper story about me, and Chelsea de Guzman's MySpace page. There were some dead Minerva Clarks, pioneer women who helped settle the West, and a girl in West Virginia named Minerva Clark who had recently won a regional spelling bee. There was no ninety-year-old Minerva Clark in Portland who raised potbellied pigs. Just as I thought, there was only one Minerva Clark in our neck of the woods, and that was me.